TAKE A CHANCE ON LOVE

Fleeing family tragedy, a new start working at Margrave Manor seems perfect to Marie. Matthew Hughes, the charming gardener, takes a shine to her, but Mrs Johnson the house-keeper resents her very presence. What's more, Mrs Johnson warns Marie that Matthew has a murky past. When the police are called to an incident, everyone falls under suspicion. Will handsome, commanding Detective Sergeant Martin solve the mystery, and could he finally be the man to mend Marie's broken heart?

Books by Cara Cooper
in the Linford Romance Library:

SAFE HARBOUR

CARA COOPER

TAKE A CHANCE ON LOVE

Complete and Unabridged

LINFORD
Leicester

First published in Great Britain in 2009

First Linford Edition
published 2009

British Library CIP Data

Cooper, Cara.
  Take a chance on love.- -
  (Linford romance library)
  1. Love stories.
  2. Large type books.
  I. Title II. series
  823.9'2–dc22

  ISBN 978–1–84782–902–3

Published by
F. A. Thorpe (Publishing)
Anstey, Leicestershire

Set by Words & Graphics Ltd.
Anstey, Leicestershire
Printed and bound in Great Britain by
T. J. International Ltd., Padstow, Cornwall

This book is printed on acid-free paper

1

Marie took the letter out of her bag again and watched the taxi speed off into the darkness. Maybe it was her imagination but he seemed super-keen to be away from this place. She held her umbrella with difficulty against the driving wind. Rain spattered off it tearing over the spidery words in her letter, threatening to make it more illegible than it already was.

Well, this was definitely the address, Margrave Manor, but she had never imagined it would be so out in the wilds. The Essex countryside probably looked great on a warm summer's day, but in the latter part of an English autumn, the bad weather whipped straight off the coast and over the flat landscape to chill the sturdiest of bones.

It would have been a help if the taxi had taken her right up to the front door, but the driver had shaken his head, 'No, Miss, I'm afraid the old lady there isn't too keen on visitors. One of our drivers got a right talking to some time ago when he got lost and called in for directions. She nearly set the dog on him she did.' It seemed Marie's new boss was a force to be reckoned with.

Marie stood by the heavy iron gates which she supposed had been left open for her arrival, sopping wet leaves blowing at her feet and took a better look at Margrave Manor. The house scowled back at her, its long windows like staring eyes. Dark green creeper dripped like tear-stained lashes.

Marie shivered. She certainly couldn't turn back at this late stage, and besides, what did she have to go back to? Nothing. Struggling to be strong, she gripped the handle of her suitcase, it contained everything she owned. She pushed her shoulders back and breathed in as she marched to the door looking far more confident than she felt, and pulled at the heavy doorbell.

'Ah, so, you've arrived then. We were expecting you much earlier than this. Your dinner's in the oven but I don't know what state it'll be in.' The woman with the short red hair and unsmiling face looked her up and down like a teacher looking at a wilful child. Marie supposed she probably did look a bit of a mess. This woman was too young to be Lady Margrave. The letter had told her that a gardener and a housekeeper were on the staff and this prickly woman was undoubtedly the latter.

'Sorry,' sputtered Marie, 'my train was cancelled and — '

'Hurry up and come in, I don't want rain and mud all over the clean floor. Shake that umbrella out in the porch before you put it in the stand.'

'Yes, of course.' After eight hours' travelling, Marie could have hoped for a nicer welcome. Down the hallway, she followed the stout woman who seemed to be made up of a series of squares. She had a square hairdo, square shoulders and a square body. The house

3

felt almost as cold inside as the air outside until Marie came to the kitchen. A large coal fired cooking range radiated heat, with a black and white collie dog sprawled in front of it. As she entered the room, the collie sat to attention and wagged his tail. Thank goodness someone's pleased to meet me thought Marie.

The older woman reached into the oven, produced a hot plate of roast dinner and unceremoniously pushed it over to Marie.

'Why, thank you very much,' Marie hastened to shrug off her wet coat. 'Really you shouldn't have bo . . . '

'I didn't,' said the other woman dismissively. 'I always do a cooked dinner for Lady Margrave. It's no trouble to put together the leftovers.'

'Right,' said Marie, 'Thank you. Um where should I put this?'

The housekeeper took her sopping coat between a finger and thumb and hung it on the back of a chair by the fire. Placing herself in a comfortably-cushioned rocking chair opposite she observed Marie who took the seat at the table. Marie would have liked to have a chance to leave her things in her room and dry out a bit but making Marie feel at ease was obviously not high on this lady's agenda.

'I suppose you'll be wondering who I am. Mrs Johnson's the name. I've been with Lady Margrave now for many years. There isn't a thing about this house or the Mistress that I don't know.'

'Pleased to meet you, Mrs Johnson. I hope we'll become firm friends,' Marie gave what she hoped was a winning smile and held out her hand. It wasn't taken.

'Hrmph,' was the reply and Marie supposed that would have to do for now. 'I'm the housekeeper here. You'll find we keep a very neat and tidy house and we like things done on time. Routine is very important to Lady Margrave.'

Marie looked around the spotless kitchen with its large oak dresser filled with white and gold rimmed china. 'It certainly looks all in apple pie order, your kitchen does you credit.'

Marie wasn't sure if her attempt at a compliment had hit home or not, as Mrs Johnson didn't reply. Mrs Johnson was leaning down to stroke the collie's head, as he rested it on her knee. 'This is Gyp, short for Gypsy. He's a good dog, well behaved and good company, but he never barks. Lady Margrave likes her peace and quiet, she can't stand barking and noise.'

Mrs Johnson had obviously appointed herself chief spokesperson for Lady Margrave, but Marie was keen to meet her employer herself. 'Is Lady Margrave here, I'd rather like to meet her?'

'Why, of course she's here. She doesn't go out hardly at all now. She's very bad on her feet but her mind's razor sharp, always has been. But she's not to be disturbed now. She got tired of waiting for you and went to her bed. Punctuality's a very important thing to Lady Margrave.'

Oh dear, thought Marie, she hadn't

really started off on the best possible footing and yet there had been absolutely nothing she could do about the cancelled train. After that all her connections had gone haywire — all in all it had been a ghastly journey.

'I'm quite tired myself, I wonder if you might show me my bedroom and perhaps I'll catch an early night too.' So saying, Marie gathered up her knife, fork and plate and purposefully went straight to the sink and washed them up. For some reason she got the impression Mrs Johnson wasn't pleased to see Lady Margrave's new companion/personal assistant.

Marie had taken the job with high hopes that it could be a new start for her and she was going to do her darndest to make it work out. From the corner of her eye, she saw Mrs Johnson standing with her arms crossed and thought she detected a reluctant look of approval from the housekeeper for tidying up her things. If part of Marie's efforts had to include making this stern woman think well of her, then so be it.

Up till now, Marie had lived all her twenty-five years with her mother and father. When her mother had died after a long illness, followed a year later by the death of Marie's father, Marie was devastated to find that her father had lived far beyond his means. In particular his gambling had got so out of hand that her parents had left her nothing and the family house had had to be sold to pay his debts.

Marie had loved her father and knew that he gambled in part as a way of dealing with his wife's illness, but it had been heartbreaking to learn just how reckless he had been. Finding she had nothing in the world, not even a roof over her head had prompted Marie to go as far away as possible to start her new life.

As Marie struggled up the stairs with her suitcase, with the sound of Gyp padding up the stairs behind her, she

noted that Margrave Manor was deco-
rated largely in sombre greens and soft
golds. Tasteful watercolours of local
country scenes lined the staircase and
on the upper landing were oils of
children and adults in various poses
whom Marie assumed were family
members. Lady Margrave obviously
had impeccable taste even though the
grandeur was rather faded. 'What other
staff does Lady Margrave employ?'
asked Marie.

'Only a gardener now, who does a
bit of handyman stuff too. You'll meet
Matthew Hughes tomorrow. He lives
in a small cottage in the grounds so
that he can be called on if Lady
Margrave needs any repairs doing. We
used to have chauffeurs too, but that
was some time ago. It's not necessary
now, Lady Margrave goes out so
seldom. She used to be out and about
a lot with all the charities she's
involved with, she was invited to the
most wonderful parties and dinners.
But it just tires her out too much

these days. Most of her dealings with the outside world are by letter. I suppose that's why she feels the need to employ you.'

This last was said with a slight sneer which made Marie think that not only did Mrs Johnson not particularly like having a stranger about, but that she disapproved of the notion of Lady Margrave needing a personal assistant at all.

Marie sighed as they finally reached the top step. She felt as if she'd been on the go for ages. Not just today, but for months, her life had been a series of upsets and disruptions. It seemed impossible that this strange old house with its established household of strangers could ever feel like home.

'Sit, Gyp,' said Mrs Johnson. 'He knows he's not allowed in here, the black hairs on his coat would shed everywhere and the last thing I need is more work.'

When Mrs Johnson opened a heavy oak door saying, 'this is your room,'

Marie could only gasp, wide-eyed as she put her suitcase down on the thick carpet.

'It's absolutely beautiful.'

'I'm glad you're impressed, you should be. For some reason, Lady Margrave's given you one of the best bedrooms in the house. She felt it had been wasted for too long now that hardly anyone comes to visit.' Mrs Johnson smoothed over the sumptuous white cover on the large double bed. The walls were papered in a rich cream and blue toile de joie paper depicting scenes of Gainsborough-like figures in long dresses, enjoying the countryside.

At the massive window, heavy cream curtains were topped with elaborate swags and tails. You couldn't have found a finer room in a palace. 'Mind you look after things in here. Most of the antiques are original, Lady Margrave doesn't care for reproductions.'

'Of course I will.' Marie peered around. In the corner a cabinet filled with little pill boxes. It was a wonderful collection. There were Christmas ones with the year printed below snow covered scenes and ones specially to mark occasions such as the Queen's Jubilee. In the opposite corner was a bookcase filled with leather covered classics. Sheer joy, thought Marie. If she got the time, she would be able to re-read all the books she had so enjoyed in her teens but which she'd been too busy to indulge in when she became old enough to go out to work.

'Well, I can't hang around here, I've got a home, a husband and a teenage daughter to get back to. I shall probably be here before you're even up in the morning. The bathroom's the second door on the right down the passage. Goodnight.'

After unpacking and placing her clothes carefully in the heavy oak wardrobe, Marie padded down the hallway to the bathroom. As she came out, she saw Gyp, lying outside a door at the far end. Apart from lifting his tail once or twice to acknowledge her presence, he seemed settled for the night. That must be Lady Margrave's room he was guarding so faithfully, thought Marie and quietly closed her door. Tomorrow, she would meet her mistress and find out whether she matched the rather strict impression Mrs Johnson had given her.

*   *   *

The next day, Marie woke early. As she lay in bed, she heard the floorboards creak above her and guessed that Mrs Johnson must be already about her chores. Marie sprang out of bed and opened the curtains. A sumptuous garden lay before her.

The central lawn was bright green after the rains of the day before and smooth as a bowling green. Either side of it were two herbaceous borders filled with late autumn chrysanthemums and dahlias in deep reds and burnished golds.

At the end of the vista, a pond, or

more like a small lake shimmered in the early sun. At the far end of the garden, staking up the odd bloom that had been bent by the rain, Marie caught sight of a tall, lean figure with dark tousled hair.

As she watched, he straightened up, stretched and yawned. Then, looking up, he caught sight of Marie and she darted quickly away from the window, embarrassed at being caught studying him. That must be Matthew Hughes.

If the rest of the house was up, she'd better get going quickly, or she'd only confirm Mrs Johnson's poor impression of her. Washing swiftly and dressing in a neat brown skirt and white shirt, Marie slipped on a brown cardigan against the early morning chill and went downstairs. Quietly she made her way to the kitchen noting that there was still no sign of her employer. When she got to the kitchen there was only Gyp there for company.

'Hello boy. That's a nice greeting, are you pleased to see me?' She stroked his silky ears and gave him a hug. His

14

warm body felt comforting and helped to alleviate her feelings of trepidation. 'Thanks for the hug, friend. I think I'm going to need all the help I can get in this place.'

As Marie searched for the kettle, she saw a short, terse note sitting beside it. *Up cleaning the rooms. Make your own breakfast.* Oh Lord, thought Marie. In a strange house, in the ultra-picky Mrs Johnson's kitchen that was a bit of a tall order. What if she broke anything or used up the last of the bread, she wouldn't be very popular then. Perhaps she would do without breakfast. But then, apart from the fact that she was ravenously hungry, if Mrs Johnson discovered she hadn't eaten, she might feel obliged to cook Marie something and Marie wanted to be as little trouble as possible.

I'll just have to be brave and go for it, she thought opening what looked like a food cupboard. It was full of bowls and plates. At least that was a start she thought taking down a plate. Opening the fridge, she decided that as there were a dozen eggs, it wouldn't spoil Mrs Johnson's housekeeping arrangements to use just two for some scrambled eggs. Gyp with his head cocked to one side seemed to approve so Marie, after opening the many cupboards and drawers managed to find herself a pan, some butter and wooden spoon.

Once the eggs were on, she felt herself to be the picture of capable organisation, and was pretty pleased with herself. It was then, she heard an agitated buzzing. At the window a huge angry wasp battered itself against the glass, then came out and flew at Marie making her jump up and yell. She'd been scared stiff of wasps ever since one had stung her as a child and given her an allergic reaction.

As she leaned and tried to open the window, she couldn't budge it and the wasp flew past her nose. 'Oh,' she cried, 'get away you horrid thing.' The back door was the only thing for it. She opened the door and after much swatting, managed to drive the wasp out. Gyp who had been running around, enjoying the sport then decided that it was his chance to escape and shot out of the door.

'Gyp, Gyp, come back,' Marie pleaded in a loud whisper. Oh no, at this rate she was going to wake Lady Margrave. Besides, was Gyp even allowed out on his own? He might get lost, or dig up all those perfect flowers. To top it all, a loud buzz in her ear signalled that the sleepy wasp had found its way back in. Then, Marie smelt the most awful whiff of burning. Turning to the pan, there were her eggs, billowing evil smelling black smoke all over Mrs Johnson's pristine kitchen.

It was a disaster, Marie didn't know whether to turn first to the eggs, the wasp or to the door to get Gyp back in. 'Heavens, what on earth's going on in here?' Deep, commanding tones came to Marie's ears, she whirled around and there with his arms on his hips staring at the chaos, stood the man she had seen from the window.

'Please help me, Gyp's escaped, I'm being attacked by a wasp . . . And oh!' This last gasp came in a panic as Marie twiddled all the knobs on the hob and couldn't work out which one sat underneath the pan of eggs.

The man finally took pity on her, strode over to the hob, turned it off and then expertly dispatched the wasp out of the window.

'Thank you,' breathed Marie staring at the smoke. 'What about Gyp?'

'He's all right, he can't get lost, there's a wall all round the garden. He might decide to go for a swim in the lake precisely because he knows he shouldn't, but it won't kill him.'

'What a mess, what on earth is Mrs Johnson going to say?'

'If we act quickly, she might never know.' His calming tone was an absolute blessing. 'I'm Matthew Hughes,' he took off his gardening glove and offered her a hand. She gratefully shook it liking his firm, confident grip.

'Very pleased to meet you, Matthew Hughes. I'm Marie Clarke.'

'So, you're the new super-efficient personal assistant.'

Marie bit her lip. 'I guess so.'

Matthew smiled and said, 'Don't look so worried. You deal with the pan, scrape that mess into a bowl and I'll get rid of some of this smoke.' Opening the window and doors wide, he twirled a tea towel in the air to push out the smoke as Marie battled with the burnt egg. At that moment Gyp bounded in, jumping up and down like a miniature kangaroo trying to bite the tea towel, enjoying what he had decided was a new game.

As Marie finally finished scouring out the saucepan, she asked, 'Is there any newspaper I can wrap this up in?' The messy egg in the bowl would surely condemn her as the culprit. 'I don't want Mrs Johnson to know, she'll think I'm terribly wasteful.'

'No need to waste it,' said Matthew and with one move, he whistled to Gyp, placed the bowl on the floor and darted out of the dog's way as he zoomed in to gobble up the crisp egg.

'He's like a canine hoover set on high speed. That dog can be trusted to eat anything,' smiled Matthew.

As if to prove him right, Gyp looked at them, licking his lips, a sparkling clean bowl at his feet.

'Have you been feeding that dog again?' Mrs Johnson's voice boomed from behind them, making Marie jump. 'You know I keep him on a strict diet, Lady Margrave doesn't want him getting fat. And what's that dreadful smell?'

'Sorry Mrs J,' said Matthew just as Marie opened her mouth to confess. He winked in her direction and said, 'I've been burning some garden waste.'

'Well, for heaven's sake, don't do it so close to the house in future.' Mrs Johnson bustled in and deposited her box of dusters and polish on the table.

'And how many times have I asked you to wipe your feet before you come in to the kitchen. Really, Matthew, that's most unlike you, now take your muddy boots back into the garden, will you?'

Flashing Marie a quick knowing smile, Matthew briefly put his finger to his lips to indicate that her recent mishap was their secret and disappeared. At least it looked as if Marie might have another friend to go with Gyp who was threatening to give the game away by sitting and looking up at her as if to ask for more tidbits.

'Lady Margrave is ready to see you now. She's in the morning room. It's the last door on the right.'

Marie quickly got up, her heart beating rapidly. She was finally to meet her boss. Already her morning had been somewhat trying. She breathed deeply, smoothed her skirt, knocked and at the brisk, 'enter,' walked in.

2

There, sitting at an imposing Maple-wood desk sat a tall, very slender lady with her grey hair coiled up in a smart chignon. She wore a deep blue high-necked dress and a row of simple, classic pearls. In her gnarled hand she held a silver-tipped cane. Marie could see that although she was lined she would at one time have been a considerable beauty. She had the grace of a ballet dancer as she stretched her long neck and looked up to greet Marie. 'Take a seat, Miss Clarke.'

Marie lowered herself into the leather-backed chair on the other side of the desk. Behind Lady Margrave were French doors leading on to a stone patio which looked out on to the garden. Marie could no longer see Matthew Hughes, but on the desk, she saw the fruits of his labour. A round bowl spilling with deep red and white late summer roses.

'Beautiful, aren't they? I couldn't live without a rose garden.'

'They are lovely. My father — ' Marie started then quickly finished, 'used to love roses.' She would have gone on to say that he had grown them, had won prizes for them but then she caught herself before she revealed too much about her circumstances. To come from a family which had been riddled with debt would, she decided, not do her much credit. A hot blush of shame suffused her neck and she hoped Lady Margrave had not noticed it.

'So, Miss Clarke,' Lady Margrave sat back in her chair and regarded Marie with her cool grey eyes, 'your CV here says you are capable of looking after a busy office.'

'That's right.' Marie took a moment to glance at the fascinating family photos on the wall.

'The duties I have for you here are a mixture of paperwork and companionship. I have to confess, for a once very active woman like myself, to be physically inactive is a curse. This leg gives me endless trouble. I have always walked with a limp ever since I came off my horse in India in my youth. But as I have grown older, it protests more, particularly with the advance of winter.' So saying, she gazed wistfully at family photos above the fireplace. 'Come girl, hold my hand and I shall show you my photos as you seem interested.'

'They look fascinating,' Marie went to Lady Margrave's side, waited as she eased herself out of the chair and then held out a steady hand for the older woman to hold. 'You have good strong bones, like I used to have. See, here, that's me on that elephant, with my brother behind me. Here we are with our ayah, they were very important ladies in the household. Our ayah was more like a mother to me than my own mother. She washed and dressed me and I spent so much of my life with her

I spoke in her language before I could even speak in English. We had a huge tea plantation and here are all the ladies with their baskets on their backs. They used to throw the leaves in after they picked them. I never realised when I was a child how much those poor women worked, from dawn until dusk sometimes.'

After they had studied all the photographs, Marie's eye was caught by a cabinet housing dozens of porcelain figurines of dogs. 'These are gorgeous,' she said.

'Aren't they? It has taken me years to acquire enough to fill this cabinet. They're all Meissen you know, very collectable. My favourite is this little chap, a collie dog with one ear up and one ear down. He reminds me a little of Gyp when he's been naughty.'

Before Marie realised it, an hour had passed and she could have listened to Lady Margrave forever, but she could see her employer was becoming tired and offered to settle her down on the sofa and get her a cup of tea. 'That would be nice my dear.'

My dear! Lady Margrave was nothing like the battleaxe she'd been expecting. Sure, she was a commanding presence and very regal, but Marie felt her employer liked her; they seemed to be getting on well together.

When Marie got to the kitchen she was pleased to see that Mrs Johnson was nowhere around. She did not know what the protocol on tea making was and the last thing she wanted to do was step on Mrs Johnson's toes.

She rushed around finding a tray, cups and saucers, sugar, and biscuits and sneaked the tray with its steaming pot quickly back to where Lady Margrave sat patiently waiting.

'Ah tea and biscuits. My goodness we never usually have biscuits with our morning tea, although I am very partial to them. Mrs Johnson usually only serves them in the afternoon. She keeps a very sure hold on the purse strings, but I appreciate her diligence. There are so many repairs to an old house like this so we have to save the pennies where we can.'

'I'm sorry, I don't want to break any rules. Would you like me to take the biscuits back?'

'Certainly not. Now you've bought them we shall have our special little treat and hope that Mrs Johnson doesn't find out.'

As they conspiratorially ate their custard creams, drinking their tea, Marie wondered whether it was perhaps Mrs Johnson who was more a stickler for rules than her employer.

As they finished their tea and Marie put aside the tray, Lady Margrave brushed an errant crumb from her skirt and said, 'We have been neglecting our duties have we not? See over there on the table, I have a pile of letters waiting to be replied to. My hands ache now when I am writing and to have someone to dictate to is such a help.'

Although Lady Margrave was advanced in years, she clearly still worked very hard. The Margrave Foundation was a small charity helping young people in India, and many of the letters updated Lady Margrave on children who had benefited from the Foundation's work. 'It's my way of putting a little back into a country that was very good to my family' Lady Margrave had explained.

Over in the corner of the room, was a cupboard with wooden double doors and hanging pockets. In each pocket, meticulously labelled was the name of the child who had benefited from The Margrave Foundation, with photographs and details of their education and the careers or businesses that many of them now ran successfully.

Marie felt a growing respect for her employer who had obviously worked tirelessly for others even though she was privileged herself. After a sandwich lunch, which the two of them ate together, Marie helped Lady Margrave upstairs to her afternoon nap. The morning had gone well, Marie took the plates and tray from morning tea into the kitchen. There sat Mrs Johnson, slicing beans. 'I would have taken tea in had you asked for it,' came her frosty greeting.

'Really it was no bother. I looked after my mother and father when they were ill, so I'm used to a few household chores.'

'Leave them on the side and I'll wash them up. I'm about to cook dinner and you shall get in the way if you try to do them now.'

Marie thought of protesting, wanting to pull her weight, but she decided better of it. They say too many cooks spoil the broth and some people were very clear what help they wanted in the kitchen and what they didn't. She got the impression the kitchen was firmly Mrs Johnson's territory and that she was largely here only by invitation. 'Well,' Marie backed out of the kitchen, 'if you're sure.'

'I'm sure.'

'Then I'll leave you to it.'

'Just one thing,' said Mrs Johnson

putting down the slicer and wiping her hands on her apron.

'Yes?'

'I noticed you talking to Matthew Hughes this morning.'

'Yes,' Marie answered, colouring slightly, 'we did introduce ourselves.'

'I'm not surprised he introduced himself to you. That young man is far too handsome and charming for his own good. He knows a pretty girl when he sees one. But make sure you don't let him turn your head. He's not all he seems to be.'

'What do you mean?'

'I'm not saying any more, I'm not one to gossip. I just thought you ought to know.' With that, she picked up a bean from the bowl in front of her and the slicer, pursed her lips and got back to her work.

As Marie walked down the passage, Gyp got up from the spot where he had been sunning himself and got up to follow her. Marie wandered up the stairs to her own room. What on earth can Mrs Johnson have meant by that? It was true; Matthew Hughes was darkly handsome, with looks a bit like a gypsy with his wild hair and haunting eyes.

As Marie opened the door to her room and patted Gyp on the head saying, 'Sorry boy, you know the rules.' She flumped down in the armchair, which overlooked the garden feeling jaded at Mrs Johnson's remarks. Matthew had seemed so nice and such fun. His dark looks and twinkling eyes were so unlike Adrian's cool grey eyes.

Adrian! She marvelled as she realised she hadn't thought of Adrian once since she'd got here. As school friends, she'd always liked him. One thing had led to another and, from going to the youth club together, they had started going to the cinema and before she knew it they were dating. Adrian had got his job in a bank and was doing well. Marie had got her job in the insurance company and it looked as if the two of them would eventually marry.

The only thing that kept getting in

the way was her mother's illness during which Marie felt she couldn't leave home. When her father then became ill, Adrian said he was happy to wait for them to begin their life together. It had been such a blow when, after her father's death, Adrian's ardour seemed to cool. First there was all the nastiness over discovering her father's debts and finding each day yet more final demands on the mat.

'I ought to distance myself a little, Marie,' Adrian had said. 'Think of my career. I'm well on the way to being a trainee bank manager. I can't be connected to anyone who has these sort of debts hanging over them.'

'But they're not my debts,' pleaded Marie.

But nothing she could say changed his mind. He suddenly stopped answering his phone when she called or, at the odd times when she did catch him, claiming he was too busy studying to go out. Then, once the debts had cleared and they were out for one of the now infrequent drinks at a local bar, she had raised the possibility of them getting together permanently.

In the past, they had talked about getting a flat together but now that she was free, he had changed his mind! It was one of the reasons Marie had come so far away. After such a betrayal, the thought of bumping into Adrian in the street, possibly with a new girlfriend made her stomach turn over. It had dawned uncomfortably on Marie that maybe the fact that she had been trapped, looking after her mother, had been part of the attraction for Adrian.

It became obvious that although he had talked about marriage at a time when she obviously had to stay at home and, when the chance came to commit, he didn't want to. He had used Marie when she was at her most vulnerable, and it had cut her like a knife. That chapter of her life was over now.

She was stronger after all she had been through. Marie allowed her eyes to wander into the garden where she saw Matthew Hughes clipping one of the box hedges. She frowned and turned away. Her new life here was what was important now, and she was determined to make a success of it.

By the next day, Marie felt she was getting much more into her stride. She was down in the morning room before Lady Margrave. 'I hope you don't mind, but I've filed the paperwork we did yesterday. If there's anything I've done wrong, you can let me know.'

Taking careful, precise steps, Lady Margrave accompanied by Gyp made her way over and congratulated Marie on her work. 'No, I can't see anything wrong. Everything looks in perfect order. You catch on very quickly.'

But as they spoke, Marie could see there was something on Lady Margrave's mind. 'Is everything all right?'

'Yes, I'm sorry I'm a little preoccupied,' Lady Margrave sat at her desk, with Gyp curled at her feet, 'I received this letter this morning.'

Marie sat down opposite her to read

it. 'It sounds like a very good cause.'

'It is. I helped to set up that school, it's in one of the poorest areas of India and they do some excellent work, but as you can see, many of their books have been destroyed in a recent fire. Stocking a whole library will cost a pretty penny but they need the new books now if the school is to continue functioning to its very high standard. I just don't know how to raise the money.'

'I've never done any fund-raising but I could do a little research and see if I can come up with some sort of grant we could apply for.'

'I don't know much about grants. In the past, if we needed to support a particular project, I would hold a fund-raising dinner and even dances in the old days but I'm a bit beyond all that preparation now. Still, let's not fret about it. This morning, because I am having one of my good days, I think we should spend some of it outside.'

Lady Margrave gripped the arm that Marie offered and pulled herself up out of the chair. 'Although I took you on as my personal assistant, I also want a companion as well. I need someone to help keep me mobile. After all, what is it you young people say, use it or lose it? We will start by taking a small tour of the garden. Open the French doors there and you can help me down the patio steps.'

The sun was bright with not a cloud in the sky; so different from the night Marie had arrived. Gyp, glad to be out, bounded across the lawn in front of them, his tail whisking back and forth.

'I used to come out here every day and tour around with our old gardener, giving him orders and selecting flowers and fruit and vegetables for the house. I must have been a real burden to him I suppose.' Lady Margrave chuckled at the memory. 'We used to entertain a lot in those days, doing loads of fund-raising dinners. I was very keen to make a good impression and our floral displays were the talk of the district. We even once held the local flower show in a marquee in this very garden. The village green was being dug up that year to lay piping, so the show was held here. What a lot of hard work it was, but I enjoyed it particularly as they asked me to be one of the judges.'

'Did that mean you got to sample all the jams and cakes? My mother was a great cake-maker.'

'I did indeed get to taste everything although I have to say, some weren't up to much.' At that point, Lady Margrave's sharp eyes focussed on Marie. 'You don't talk much about your parents.'

Marie looked down. 'They died fairly recently and the memory of them is still a little too fresh in my mind.'

'I'm sorry I intruded on your grief. Forgive me.'

Marie was reluctant to talk about her parents mainly because of the shame her father had brought on the family. She was unhappy at having to deceive Lady Margrave into thinking it was just sadness which made her reluctant to reveal more. But, this job was vitally important to her, she couldn't risk anyone finding out about the trouble her family had got into.

She had always been ultra reliable and managed her finances impeccably, but it had been a real problem sorting out all the debts her father had left. Marie had certainly found that Lady Margrave was far more easy to get on with than Mrs Johnson had lead her to believe, and many of the qualms she had had on her first night had evaporated. Marie looked at the wonderful garden and basked in the thought of how lucky she was to have found this job in its beautiful surroundings.

'I have arranged to meet Matthew Hughes so that he can show us around. You have met him, I believe.'

Marie's heart did a little skip at his name. She had not seen him since that first day, but she found her eyes roaming over the garden whenever she looked out of the window, wondering if she would see him.

'Yes, I have met him once,' Marie dare not tell Lady Margrave about the incident in the kitchen. It would have done nothing to preserve the impression Marie wished to present of an efficient personal assistant.

'He will be in the greenhouse today. He's been busy recently potting up cuttings of all the tender perennials.'

They went behind a tall conifer hedge at the end of the garden and there stood a long greenhouse. As they went in, the heat hit them. Gyp installed himself in the corner under a bench and panted, his pink tongue sticking out. 'I used to love coming in here on a chilly day,' confided Lady Margrave. 'I think I used to drive the gardeners mad — we had three then — getting in their way. But even if it was windy outside it was always warm in here.'

Along the benches little pots of healthy cuttings of geraniums, fuchsias and chrysanthemums stood in rows all neatly labelled. 'Isn't it wonderful and orderly, Matthew is one of the tidiest men I know.'

At the end, his head bent downwards in concentration stood Matthew Hughes. He looked up as they approached and tossed aside his head to get his floppy fringe out of his eyes. What eyes they were too. Marie had noticed their rich brown intensity the other day. She was fascinated by the contrast in Matthew Hughes. Wild and untamed in his looks, but incredibly orderly in his work. He smiled and Marie smiled back.

'Ah, Miss Clarke,' he said, a wicked glint in his eye. 'Been doing any more cooking lately.'

Marie narrowed her eyes and parried his remark saying, 'No, I leave most of that to Mrs Johnson. I think a simple bowl of cereal and milk in the morning is safer.'

Their easy banter didn't escape the notice of Lady Margrave who wore the expression of someone pleased to see youthful high spirits around her once again, even if she wasn't quite sure what the joke was about.

She wagged a finger at her jovial gardener, in the manner of a Victorian governess, 'I hope you're not leading Miss Clarke astray, Matthew, she's here to keep us all in line, although I know any woman would have a hard time keeping you in check.'

'Lady Margrave,' with a winning smile, he held out a freshly-cut rose bud to her which she accepted for her buttonhole, 'you're the only woman who's ever managed to keep me in check.'

'Humbug,' she chided although he had brought a delightful smile to her face. Mrs Johnson had been right. He certainly was a charmer. 'Now come on and show us around your domain, I want Marie to have a better idea of how the house and garden work.'

They spent a very pleasant morning wandering along the herbaceous border listening to Matthew relate how he had planned the colour scheme so that the colours blended one into another and didn't clash. Gyp tagged along with them, sniffing at interesting plants and sitting occasionally in the sun.

As Matthew talked, Marie couldn't help noticing how boyish his unruly hair was, and how deliciously it curled about his tanned neck. She hadn't looked at another man since Adrian had so cruelly let her down, but there was something about Matthew Hughes, which had captured her imagination. He was light-hearted with Lady Margrave while still being respectful and Marie could imagine that he was one of the few people whose charm was such that he could be a bit cheeky with the old lady and get away with it.

Every now and then, as Marie felt herself falling under his spell, Mrs Johnson's words came back to haunt her. 'He's not all he seems to be.' What on earth could she mean by that? The words jarred on Marie's consciousness. Maybe his easy charm was something she should fear.

For now though, she was simply enjoying listening to Matthew and Lady Margrave's easy conversation. Both of them were passionate about plants. 'The turquoise delphiniums were a picture in the summer Matthew. Did you take cuttings?'

'Yes, I did. We should be able to have a second bed next year. They went particularly well against the Iceberg roses I thought. Did you like that combination, Lady Margrave?'

'It was wonderful. You have a real talent with colour.'

'Thank you, Lady Margrave.' Marie saw him bask in his employer's praise, and every now and then he would put out a gentle hand to steady her progress across the lawn. Mrs Johnson may have reservations about him, but all Marie could see was his kindness and respect for their elderly employer.

They then came to a square, walled section of the garden which took Marie's breath away. As they entered through a red brick arch, the scent of roses was overpowering. Each wall was densely covered in red, white and pink roses. In the centre of the square was a bower with a seat at its centre. Climbing shell pink roses dropped down in between the bower, it would be the perfect place to sit on a warm evening. Standard roses stood outside the bower in the most stunning shade of blood red.

'I think I shall sit here a while and catch my breath. Come on Gyp, you sit with me and keep an old lady company.' Lady Margrave sighed as she settled herself down on to the wooden bench to enjoy the scent. Gyp lay at her feet, resting his muzzle on his paw. 'Why don't you give Marie a guided tour of your wonderful roses, Matthew?'

He had recently had Lady Margrave hanging on to his arm and this time, he held it out for Marie to take. She didn't need supporting, but felt a tiny electric thrill run up her hand as she felt his warm tanned skin under her fingers.

'You like roses then?'

'I think they are the queen of all the flowers. My father used to grow a wonderful, wonderful rose. Its scent was like wine. I wish I could remember its name.'

'What colour was it?'

'The deepest of reds. Almost black in bud.'

'Might it have been Deep Secret?'

'That was it. You're so clever when it comes to plants.'

'Only when it comes to plants I'm afraid. I was thrown out of school for behaving badly, but you don't have to be clever to remember something you're very fond of. Deep Secret is one of my favourites.'

As they wandered, Marie's hand lightly resting on his arm, he pointed out to her the old gallica roses, some of which were centuries old and then the new English roses which had all the charm of the old roses but which flowered all the season. There was very little he didn't know about growing them and even explained to her how new varieties were bred.

'When Lady Margrave held a lot of parties here, this was one of her favourite places for the guests to take early evening drinks. I'm glad you've seen it now, sometimes months pass with no visitors apart from the birds and the butterflies. It's sad because late summer is the best time in this garden. Many of the plants are into their second and last flush. The blooms are less showy than the early summer ones but, like women when they mature, they have more depth to them and are twice as beautiful for it.'

He said this a little wistfully and Marie realised that Matthew was like an artist painting canvasses which were rarely on display. Then, a thought struck Marie in relation to the conversation she and Lady Margrave had had earlier about the school which needed money for books. She would sit down with a pen and paper when she got back to the house and work out her idea so she could present it to Lady Margrave.

As they helped Lady Margrave up and made their way back across to the house, Matthew said, 'and the last part of my domain, as Lady Margrave calls it, is the wood store. We keep the logs and the coal here for the open fires in the winter. See here, next to the kitchen, it has a door into the garden and one into the house which I never use.'

'Mrs Johnson would tick me off until my ear ached if I trod coal dust on to her precious hallway carpet. But as well as keeping all the logs in here for the winter, I keep this shelf of clay pots. Some of these are almost as old as the house. The long toms are for things like sweet peas.'

Marie admired rows of neatly stacked and carefully cleaned pots. They came out of the wood store and went back on to the lawn. As they walked around to the French doors, their quiet stroll was intruded upon by Mrs

Johnson running out of the house in an uncharacteristic flap, her heavy brows knitted with concern. She shooed Gyp inside the house, sending him off to the kitchen with his tail between his legs.

'Is there something wrong, Mrs Johnson?'

'Yes, Lady Margrave, something is very wrong. We've been burgled.'

3

'Burgled? What do you mean? I can't believe this!' They all made their way back into the house.

'Come and see,' Mrs Johnson was breathless with panic.

Marie caught Matthew's eye and saw a hard expression that she found difficult to reconcile with his previous jovial warmth. Mrs Johnson led them into the morning room and pointed to the cabinet with the Meissen dogs which Marie had admired only a day or so ago.

'See,' Mrs Johnson pointed frantically to the figures. 'The Dalmatian has gone, completely disappeared. I noticed it as soon as I started dusting them.'

Lady Margrave looked most concerned and peered inside. 'Are you sure? Could you perhaps have taken the dogs out and forgotten to put one back?'

'Certainly not,' said Mrs Johnson looking most offended. 'I'm sorry, my Lady but I've been dusting those figurines for years now, I've watched that collection grow and anything I take out of that cabinet I'm always sure to put back, exactly where it came from.'

'Of course you are,' Lady Margrave's expression was one of grave concern. 'I didn't mean to imply you weren't doing your job, but I know how busy you are and how sometimes the doorbell rings or the phone goes when one is in the middle of something and it's easy to get confused.'

'Well, I've never been confused before and I'm not about to be now. No ma'am, someone's stolen it.' Her eyes then roamed towards first Matthew Hughes and then Marie. Marie gasped as she felt a hint of suspicion fall on her. She was the one who had only just arrived, and she had been admiring the figurines only recently. The unsaid words hung in the silence like thunder.

Lady Margrave must have picked up on the tension and was having none of it, for she quickly said, 'If we really think there has been some foul play, the correct course of action is to telephone the police. Please could you do that, Marie?' Marie could have been imagining it, but she sensed that being fair was central to Lady Margrave's values whereas jumping to easy conclusions was the sort of thing Mrs Johnson was more than capable of.

'I'm going to have a look around,' Matthew's usually jovial voice was suddenly serious. Marie opened her mouth and wanted to say be careful but he was out of the room in a flash.

Once she had phoned the police, Lady Margrave took charge. 'Please do us a nice pot of tea, Mrs Johnson, and I'm sure we can sit down with the police and find a rational explanation for all this.'

Mrs Johnson and Marie sat waiting

for them in the kitchen while the kettle boiled.

Marie sat threading her hands one over the other, terrified at the implication of the threat to her livelihood. Being the latest arrival on the staff, she was sure to come under the most suspicion. After all, Mrs Johnson had been here years and Lady Margrave had told her that Matthew Hughes had been here as a young lad which must have been a long time. Naturally, with only a few days service, the blame could fall on Marie.

But then, as she was pouring boiling water on to the teabags and setting cups and saucers on the tray, Mrs Johnson said something, which jolted Marie out of her personal worries. 'Between you and me,' she said sotto voce, 'I often wonder about that Matthew Hughes.'

'What do you mean?'

'You don't know Matthew like I do. He's got something of a chequered history. Back when he was a young lad, he got in with a very bad crowd in the village. There was high spirits and even some vandalism, a disrespect for people's property and one of the lads even ended up in a teenage institution. I'm not saying Matthew was a ringleader but he was definitely hanging around with undesirables. They say you can't teach an old dog new tricks and I reckon Matthew's always been a bit on the edge.'

'But surely you don't imagine he would start stealing from Lady Margrave.' Marie thought back to how considerate he had been to their employer. He would have to be a very good actor to be so two-faced and Marie simply didn't want to feel that badly towards him.

'We can all do desperate things where money is involved.' Mrs Johnson's stern face was set like a stone as she picked up the tray and marched out.

They were all summoned to the morning room. Marie and Mrs Johnson sat on one sofa with Matthew Hughes and the two policemen opposite them while Lady Margrave sat in her usual higher chair. Marie noticed her employer's knuckles white as she gripped her cane. That was the only outward sign that she was anything other than her usual composed self, but Marie felt sorry that she should be stressed by this unpleasantness.

They each sat with cups of tea and the air lay heavy about them.

'I'm Detective Sergeant Sam Martin. This is my partner, Rick Ash. Now, what's this about a disappearing antique.'

Mrs Johnson launched into her account of the lost figurine while the two policemen listened intently. 'So you can be sure that the item is actually missing and isn't simply mislaid somewhere in the house.'

'I know every inch of this house, top to bottom detective sergeant. I wouldn't get a thing like that wrong. It's definitely gone.'

'And you say you've looked around the outside and there's no sign of any forced entry.'

'Not that I can see,' proclaimed Matthew.

'And you only arrived here to work a few days ago, Miss Clarke?'

'That's right.' Marie perched on the edge of her seat, uncomfortably aware of the detective sergeant's intense gaze on her and the way his assistant took down every word people were saying. Marie smoothed her skirt nervously while the detective sergeant asked them all what seemed to be endless questions.

Finally the interview was over. 'With your permission, Lady Margrave, I shall look around the house and grounds and check for anything untoward,' Sam Martin said, standing. He was a tall, imposing man with sandy blond hair. 'Rick, I would like you to go with Lady Margrave as she says she has a photograph of the piece that has been stolen.'

As they all filtered away, Marie realised she had left her cardigan in the greenhouse and hurried back. Once she had found it, and was preparing to make her way back to the house, she suddenly jumped, seeing a figure at the far end near the door. 'I'm sorry to startle you.' It was DS Martin. 'I wanted to have a word alone with you, Miss Clarke.'

Marie's heart was still racing from her fright and she held her hand to her chest to still the beating. 'I'm sorry to be so jittery, it's just that this is all so horrid.' She tried to still the gloomy thought that her nervousness might immediately made him think she was guilty in some way.

'I can understand how difficult this is for you. I just wanted to let you know, confidentially that we do not consider you to be a suspect.'

'You don't.' Her mood immediately lightened.

'No. Frankly I wasn't overly surprised to get the call today that something had disappeared. We had a call some weeks ago, long before you arrived, that someone was seen lurking around the grounds of Margrave Manor. We immediately telephoned Lady Margrave and told her privately of the report. Not wanting to alarm the whole household she and ourselves decided to keep things quiet. This, however, is a worrying development and both Mrs Johnson and Matthew Hughes are still under suspicion until such time that we find out what all this is about.'

'Oh dear.'

'But as the other incident happened before you were appointed to Margrave Manor, Lady Margrave asked that I let you know you are in the clear to put your mind at rest. It will also help her to know that there is someone to act as a second pair of eyes and ears. You will tell us if you hear or see anything suspicious won't you?'

'Of course I will.'

DS Martin helped Marie on with her cardigan. 'There was really nothing to worry about was there?'

He had a protective manner about him which was comforting and a very winning smile when he chose to use it. But Marie noted that his touch sent nothing like the thrill Matthew Hughes's had through her frame. 'I will look around the grounds a little more, Miss Clarke, and let you get back to your work. I'm sure we'll be seeing each other again. Oh, and by the way please call me Sam.'

Marie nodded, walked on her way, and as she glanced back, felt DS Martin's eyes still on her as she returned to the house.

Once Mrs Johnson had brought their tea on a tray, and left the morning room, she and Lady Margrave discussed the disappearance of the figurine and Marie said she would be as discreet as possible, but inform DS Martin if she saw anything which might be useful to his investigation. As they were finishing their tea, Sam Martin knocked on the door.

'I'm sorry to say I haven't found any evidence of false entry on the grounds or anywhere around the house. It looks as if the thief was either here on the premises or was let in by someone here.'

Lady Margrave let Sam Martin out with a long look on her face. Her employer was clearly worried, but then Marie remembered her fund-raising idea and resolved to put it to Lady Margrave. If nothing else it would help her employer to forget her domestic difficulties.

'Looking around the garden this morning, Lady Margrave, it occurred to me that an awful lot of ordinary people in the village and surrounding towns must be curious to know what the gardens behind the walls of Margrave Manor look like. I was thinking that we could open the gardens over a weekend and use the admission fees to send to the school in India.'

She showed Lady Margrave the figures she had jotted down on a notepad. 'If we were lucky with the weather we could collect quite a lot at the door. If Matthew had some spare cuttings we could sell, people would surely buy them — his plants look so wonderful at the moment. Also, if Mrs Johnson wanted to do some baking and freeze some cakes before hand we could offer tea and cakes. I would be happy to help her. That way we would involve everybody and no-one would feel left out.'

'That's extremely thoughtful of you, Marie. It will do something to help allay my concerns about this beastly thieving of my figurine. I don't know what to think about it all.' She sighed. 'We've been a nice comfortable unit over recent years, Matthew, Mrs Johnson and I. We used to have a lot more staff and I wasn't always close to them but I have been close to my housekeeper and my gardener. I find it hard to believe that either of them had anything to do with the theft but I know if finances are difficult, people can get desperate.'

'Your idea is an excellent one. Mrs Johnson is always baking and we tend to have a freezer full of cakes anyway. I do my best to get through them but my appetite isn't what it used to be. I sometimes think Mrs Johnson is living a bit in the past when we were always having people for tea. She might even enjoy a bit of light entertaining for a change.'

'If you think it's a possibility we could arrange it for two weeks' time. That would give me enough time to distribute leaflets and have a small ad put in the local paper. The garden will still look fabulous and they've been talking about an Indian summer in the weather forecast.'

Lady Margrave chuckled, warming to the idea. 'How appropriate, an Indian summer garden opening to help an Indian school. I'll let you design the leaflet on that computer laptop thing of yours, Marie. I think we ought to splash out a bit and move into the technological age. How about us getting a colour printer, that should make the leaflets more eye catching?'

'That would be wonderful. With

Matthew's help I could also make up some sheets with photos of the plants we are selling in bloom and some instructions for growing them.'

'Perhaps Detective Sergeant Martin would distribute some leaflets from the police station too.' Marie detected a playfulness in Lady Margrave's tone when she mentioned DS Martin which made Marie wonder if her employer's suggestion was perhaps as much inspired by her wish to match-make as to promote the fund-raiser.

Marie was delighted that Lady Margrave was warming to her idea. She ordered the printer and set about producing the leaflets. She was uncertain how Mrs Johnson might view the project but, surprisingly, she showed enthusiasm for it from the start, as did Matthew. Marie hoped it would do something to warm Mrs Johnson towards her after her initial frosty reception.

'I make a fair Victoria sponge, even if I do say so myself,' Mrs Johnson sat down to write out her shopping list. 'I can do some lemon drizzle cakes as well. It's a long time since I've had to do a batch of baking and I can fill the freezer up.'

'I think it's an excellent idea,' Matthew Hughes was watering the plants in the greenhouse from a large metal watering can. Marie had gone to see him, to make a list of all the plants that would be for sale. 'I always do too many cuttings so if we can sell some to help Lady Margrave's children abroad so much the better. I could even do some bunches of cut flowers. They should go well.'

'That would be fantastic. People like to have something to take away with them when they visit a garden. I would like to display the plants for sale with a small poster by each one showing a photograph of it in bloom and giving some cultural instructions.'

Matthew suddenly looked concerned. 'I'd love to do that for you, but I'm afraid I'm no good on a computer.'

'Oh, I didn't mean for a second to

impose on you. If we could just take some time to sit down together, you can tell me what to put and I'll take notes.'

Matthew thought for a second. 'Why don't you come around to the cottage tonight and I can have a go at cooking you supper? I'm not very good but I can usually rustle up some pasta.'

Marie felt herself blush. The thought of being confined alone with Matthew Hughes set her pulse racing but then again, it wasn't a date was it? It was just the two of them getting together to work on the fund-raiser. 'That would be great, I'll bring the laptop and I can type the notes straight on to it.'

'My cottage is accessed from the drive on the west side of the house. You'll see a beaten up old red Mazda car under the trees. That's mine, just follow it and you'll come to the cottage. See you around seven o'clock.' Matthew gave her a broad smile which told her how pleased he was with the arrangement.

4

Marie did her best not to read anything into Matthew's offer. He was just being friendly and it made sense for them to sit down to do the plant notes together. Nevertheless, as she was working on the leaflets and seeing to Lady Margrave's post, her mind often strayed to what she was going to wear for the evening.

In the end, she chose a short-sleeved deep green velvet dress with a matching cardigan. A touch of peach lip gloss and a brush of mascara and she decided she was ready.

'You look radiant my dear,' said Lady Margrave as she passed her on the stairs, Gyp following closely behind. 'I'm pleased you're getting out of the house for the evening. You should get to know the area a bit, and Matthew's cottage is a lovely old listed building. Enjoy yourself.'

* * *

The narrow driveway up to Matthew's cottage was lined with blackberry bushes and plum trees and it was one of those early evenings in autumn, which are golden and calm. Marie carried her laptop in one hand and a bottle of red wine in her other which Matthew received gratefully as he opened the door.

He looked clean and smart in a white shirt and dark trousers, so different from his gardening gear. As Marie walked in, she smelt the spicy scent of his aftershave.

'A merlot, my favourite. You look really lovely this evening; your hair suits you like that. Just let me open this to breathe and I'll be right with you.'

The cottage was absolutely charming. Marie put down the laptop, and stood in a lounge with comfortable chintz sofas and a large white rug. The walls were lined with books about gardening and cars, which seemed to be

Matthew's two big passions. In the corner of the room, Marie noticed a cluster of photographs of Matthew as a child with a kindly looking couple who must have been his parents. Another showed him as a teenager with a different woman who was not old enough to be a grandmother and who was maybe an aunt.

Listening to Matthew clunking around in the kitchen, Marie wandered over to a patio door which lead out into a Victorian conservatory. Inside it, Matthew was growing lemon trees and richly-scented jasmine. A small table was laid up with cutlery and serviettes and Marie was touched to see how much effort he had gone to.

'Will a glass of white do you as an aperitif?' asked Matthew.

'That would be lovely.' Marie sipped the chilled liquid. Suddenly, she jumped, nearly spilling her wine.

'What's up,' Matthew enquired.

Marie felt her hand shaking. 'There's a huge spider over there, it was running in my direction. I'm sorry, it's just that I have a bit of a phobia about spiders. I always think they're going to run across my feet and up my leg. Look, look there it is again.' Marie tried to stem the sound of terror in her voice. She knew she was overreacting, but she couldn't help it.

'Hey,' he said kindly. 'Don't worry about it. I'll sort it out.' Going into the kitchen, he came back with a wide-necked glass, crept up on the spider and popped the glass over the top of it. Sliding a postcard underneath, he tossed the spider out of the window. 'There, are you OK?'

'Yes, thanks for being understanding. I'm such an idiot.'

'No you're not. We all have our likes and dislikes.'

Feeling much calmer after his kind words she said, 'this is such a sweet cottage.'

'You wouldn't believe how long I spent clearing it up. If you'd have come two hours earlier, it looked as if a bomb had hit it.' Matthew joked.

'How long have you lived here?'

'Over ten years. Lady Margrave was very kind to me.' He motioned to Marie to sit down on the sofa and sat at the other end, his long legs crossed in front of him as he twirled the stem of the glass in his hand. 'I was brought up by my parents until the age of fifteen when they died in a car accident. It was a terrible blow, but I was lucky enough to have an aunt in the village that looked after me.'

'The only trouble was, she was single and worked full time, so there was no-one to keep a proper eye on me. I took up with some lads from the village that I thought were great. But they weren't. There was a lot of trouble and I know my aunt was terribly worried about me.'

'She noticed Lady Margrave was advertising for an extra lad for the garden and pleaded with her to take me on. It was the making of me I suppose. When she said I could live in the cottage for a nominal rent I leapt at it. I was eighteen then and I've been here ever since.'

That confirmed what Mrs Johnson had said of Matthew. But far from his early misdemeanours making Marie suspect him more, she found that she was impressed that after suffering tragedy and getting into trouble at a young age, he had pulled himself up and learnt from his mistakes. That took some gumption and strength of character. Surely he couldn't be the one who had stolen from Lady Margrave.

As they spoke, Marie could smell a lasagne cooking in the tiny kitchen. 'Do you want a hand with anything?' she asked.

'No,' he went off to check the oven, 'it's all in control.'

When Matthew came back with a bowl of green salad to place on the table, he sat and they talked a bit more about the garden, about Marie's home and about the cars Matthew loved. 'You probably saw my beaten up old car on the driveway. I desperately need to get it fixed, there's so much wrong with it, but money's tight as always.'

As he continued, Marie felt a frisson of worry spike at her. That could be a motive for someone taking one of the dog figurines. It must be very easy, she thought, if you are surrounded by small items of great value to be tempted if you were desperate. She drove the thought out of her mind. She would leave any detective work to DS Sam Martin, he was the expert. Besides, it would hardly be fair, when Matthew had invited her into his home, to be spying on him and jumping to conclusions.

The evening drifted on in a very relaxed way. They sat down and Marie typed up the information Matthew gave her about the various plants he was going to sell.

Once their work was done, Matthew made Marie welcome in every way, topping up her glass, pulling out her chair when they sat down to eat and checking that she was comfortable.

After they had eaten what was a superb lasagne, he said he had something to show her and invited her out into his small garden. By this time there was a full moon out. 'There,' he said, spreading his arms wide. 'This is my *piece de resistance*, my white garden.'

'It's absolutely stunning,' she breathed.

There, from every corner nodding low or standing tall were the most magnificent blooms all of the purest white or richest cream. White cactus flowered dahlias stood tall next to cream pompom dahlias and white chrysanthemums looked brilliant under the moon. Marie cast her eyes in wonder, catching the scent of a white datura on the gentle breeze.

'I'm glad you like it,' beamed Matthew proudly. 'It's my antidote to the outside world. It's no surprise to me that paradise is always pictured as a garden, and I think a white garden is a place of particular peace and tranquillity. We all have our troubles don't we, but when I feel mine getting to me, I come out here and everything seems brighter.'

'I'd never have believed a garden with just one colour could look this good,' marvelled Marie.

'It looks particularly good just at dusk or under the moonlight.' Matthew turned to her, took her shoulders gently in his hands and planted the lightest of kisses on her waiting lips.

Marie gasped with surprise as her stomach flipped. Matthew's voice was low and gravely, 'I'm so glad you could come tonight, you look gorgeous standing there, like some sort of goddess. I couldn't resist kissing you.'

Matthew accompanied Marie back to the big house, planting a kiss on her cheek as he left her at the front door. Marie felt she barely needed to walk up the stairs, she was floating on air. In a dream, Marie got changed for bed and, after reading a chapter of her book was ready to settle down. She lay there wondering what Matthew's kiss had meant. Some people were just very tactile, and gestures like that carried no weight with them. She had a feeling Matthew was what would be described as a bit of a flirt.

As she lay thinking over her extraordinary evening she was suddenly distracted. She had noticed earlier that the kitchen light was on, and had heard Mrs Johnson washing up in the kitchen, but now, she thought she heard voices, and raised voices at that.

Marie got up and opened the window quietly. As her bedroom was above the kitchen, she tried to catch what was being said. It was impossible to make out the actual words but it was clear two people were having a difference of opinion, and that they were both women. There was Mrs Johnson's low mature voice, and a much younger woman's voice.

Not sure whether she should get back into bed and ignore it, or go down and see if there was anything she could do, Marie decided in the end that she ought to check things out to see if she needed to intervene.

She slipped her warm dressing gown on over her nightie and made her way into the passage. Gyp was at his usual station, outside Lady Margrave's door, and Marie got the impression that he must have known Mrs Johnson's visitor as he seemed entirely unbothered by the voices wafting up the staircase.

As Marie made her way across the landing and down the first few stairs, she thought she heard the younger woman say, 'It's just not fair, Mum.' Then, Marie tripped on her dressing gown and lost her footing, grabbing the rail noisily for support. She only fell a few steps, managing to save herself, but stubbed her toe and rubbed at the painful spot. Gyp had come to look at her from the top of the stairs. Once he assured himself all was well, he padded back to his old spot. Now, Marie noticed that the voices had stopped.

She made her way swiftly down to the kitchen, opened the door, and was just in time to see Mrs Johnson letting a young woman with blonde hair out of the back door of the kitchen and out of the side exit.

Before Marie had a chance to see the young woman clearly, Mrs Johnson had hastily shut the door. 'I'm sorry, Mrs Johnson, but I thought I heard voices. It's terribly late. Are you OK?'

'Of course I am.' She looked flustered. 'That was just my teenage daughter. It's no concern of anybody else's. She's gone back home now. Goodnight, Miss Clarke. I'm just about to lock up before I leave.' There was nothing for Marie to do but leave her to it. Nevertheless, she wondered what all the fuss had been about.

The next day brought a terrible blow as Lady Margrave announced in the morning that a small but valuable watercolour had disappeared from its place in the study. Again the police were called and again, they found no sign of anyone breaking into the house.

'It's a complete mystery,' Sam Martin

told Marie after he had interviewed everybody. When she had managed to catch him alone, she had told him about Mrs Johnson's daughter and, as he was getting into his car to go, he confided in Marie.

'Sadie Johnson has always given her mother and father problems. She's a good-looking girl that one but she has a tendency to enjoy the high life a bit too much. She's well known around the bars and pubs in the villages and she's never without some boyfriend, usually the sort with flash cars and more money than sense. Between you and me, she goes from one relationship to another and they nearly always end in tears. I suspect that was what you heard them discussing last night.'

'It sounded more like an argument than a discussion.'

'Mrs Johnson's always been too strict with the girl. Now she's a young woman, she does what she wants, but then she always comes back crying on her mother's shoulder and asking to be taken back in again. I understand she's living with Mr and Mrs Johnson again at the moment but if I know Sadie she'll be off again soon. I wouldn't be surprised if her mother was laying down some sort of ultimatum but knowing Sadie she won't change.'

'Mrs Johnson's always so abrupt with me, I never thought I'd feel sorry for her, but I do now.'

'She's used to it I reckon,' said Sam. 'Now, you be sure and bring those leaflets for the fund-raiser over when you've printed them out, won't you?'

'Of course I will, it should be in the next few days.'

'I finish about 6 p.m., if you bring them down to the station then, I can take them around to The Lamb on my way home.'

Sam had offered to persuade a local publican to display the leaflets for the fund-raiser as he reckoned that was the quickest way to spread the word.

In a couple of days the leaflets were ready. Marie took the bus to the police station which was in the nearby town. As she got off the bus, she stopped off to buy a few stationery items and call in at the post office to post a parcel for Lady Margrave on her way to the police station.

As she stood in one of the two queues for the counter, her mind suddenly clicked into gear when she heard the post office lady behind the desk say, 'Hello Sadie, how are you?'

Looking discreetly sideways, Marie noticed a young woman with bright blonde hair, straightened and sleek leaning forward on to the counter. She wore too much makeup and her red dress was so tight, she looked as if she had been poured into it.

'I'm OK. Dad's been giving me grief lately, about the usual.' She giggled. 'But I'm hoping to move out soon.'

'I thought you were moving out a while ago,' said the lady behind the till as she tore stamps out of a book.

'I was, but it all fell through. My boyfriend and me split up, but I'm going out with a really nice bloke now even though my dad doesn't like him much. But then he doesn't have to go out with him, does he?'

'You should settle down, Sadie, I don't know where you get all your energy from.'

'I will settle down some time, but I'm very choosy you know.'

Marie watched Sadie Johnson click her way out of the post office on her high heels. She certainly looked the sort of girl who would be hard work to contain.

Once Marie had got her bits and pieces, she found the police station and asked the constable at the desk to call DS Martin on the telephone.

'Really, I didn't want to disturb him, I just needed to drop those off.'

'Not at all Miss Clarke,' said the constable. 'He particularly said he wanted to see you when you called.'

5

Marie sat on the chair in the waiting area and wondered what DS Martin needed to see her about. As he came down the stairs, he looked smart, if a little stiff in a charcoal grey suit, white shirt and mauve tie.

'Nice to see you again,' he shook her hand warmly. 'I'm just about to go off duty. Let me take you for a quick drink at The Lamb. You can meet Gerald, the publican, and a few of the locals and promote the fund-raiser while you're there.'

Marie consulted her watch. She'd nearly finished her work for the day, and it would be good to get as many local people as possible interested in the fund-raiser. 'Thanks, that would be nice.'

Sam Martin was a careful driver and, while he nodded to various people who waved back, as he made his way along the narrow village streets, Marie realised he must be a well-known figure in the community.

'Sam, great to see you,' the publican at The Lamb shook Sam Martin's hand.

'This is Marie Clarke, Lady Margrave's new personal assistant up at the Manor.'

'Pleased to meet you, Miss Clarke. And thank you for bringing Sam in to see us. He's usually working too hard to take time off, but obviously he's made an exception for you.'

'I don't think it's anything to do with me,' Marie protested although she was sure she saw Gerald give Sam a wink as he poured him a half pint.

'I wouldn't be so sure. Sam used to be a regular here until he got his promotion and started spending every night at the station. Now, what can I get you, young lady?'

Marie ordered a dry white wine and noticed that, despite his protests, the publican wouldn't let Sam pay. 'It's on the house,' he said.

They sat down next to a log fire in the corner, which was welcome, as the day had turned chilly.

'It's nice to see some new blood around here,' announced Sam as he took his first sip of beer.

'It's nice for me to be in a new area.' Marie told him a bit about her parents and the fact that they were both dead. She even confessed about her father's bad debts thinking that it was best if she were totally up front with Sam about her past. Before she knew it, not only had they finished their drinks, but the publican Gerald was bringing another drink over. He also had a plate of sandwiches garnished with salad and crisps. 'All on the house,' he said, waving away any protests.

'You must be pretty well thought of here to be fed for nothing,' Marie remarked.

'I guess so,' Sam said modestly, offering her a sandwich. 'Most businesses like to befriend the local police. Besides it's no good trying to police an area if you only go there when there's trouble. You get a lot further if you get to know the people and spend time chatting to them.'

'You certainly seem to know most people round here.'

'I was born and brought up in a local village, many of my old school friends own businesses nearby. I've been asking around the local antique dealers to make sure that if either the stolen dog figurine or the painting turn up, they'll let me know. It's a long shot because often criminals will sell stuff on up in London. But, you never know, some criminals might be stupid enough to try and offer stolen goods locally. They're not always known for their high IQ.'

'Well, I hope to goodness you catch whoever it is.' And I hope, thought Marie silently, that you find it's no one connected with anyone in the household. Seeing Sadie Johnson this morning had given Marie food for thought. She looked like the sort of girl who didn't mind too much about the company she kept. It would be easy for her to get hold of a key for Margrave Manor, and she knew the back way in.

Goodness, I'm letting my imagination run away with me thought Marie as Sam's voice brought her back to the present.

'Anyway, tell me all about this fund-raiser you're doing.'

He was easy company and before she knew it, the evening had worn on. Sam had introduced her to quite a few people and all her leaflets were gone now. Most people said they'd look forward to seeing the gardens at Margrave Manor and Marie got more of an idea of the sort of numbers they might have to cater for on the day. Marie had been so engrossed, chatting with Sam, she suddenly looked at her watch and realised how late it was getting. 'I must hurry and get the bus,' she said gathering her things together.

'Nonsense, I'll drive you back to the

Manor,' Sam insisted as they got up. 'I wouldn't hear of you getting the bus.'

He drove a lovely top of the range car, which probably came with the job. As they coasted along and Marie spread out her legs in front of her thinking how smooth and roomy the car was, she felt a pang of sadness for Matthew. He would have loved a car like this; in fact he would have loved any car as long as it ran properly.

'Thank you for a lovely evening,' Marie stood on the gravel driveway of the Manor.

'Thank you. I really enjoyed your company, Marie. I hope we can do something again sometime. I'll give you a call if that's OK.' He took one of her hands in his and squeezed it, but she drew it away, anxious for him not to get the wrong impression. She liked him, but there was little spark there. Rushing into the house, Marie quickly shut the door behind her.

The next day, while she was in the morning room, phoning around to let people including the local press know about the garden opening, Marie picked up the phone only to hear Sam Martin's voice. 'Sam, hello.'

Lady Margrave looked up from the document she was reading, and then lowered her eyes again.

Sam's voice was slightly hesitant. 'There's a classical concert on at the local arts centre tomorrow night. I've been given two spare tickets by one of the lads here, as he can't go. I hope you might consider going with me.'

Marie loved classical music and it was a long time since she'd been for a proper evening out. Sam was very good company and after pondering for a second she agreed to go. He would pick her up and drop her back he said.

'That was Sam Martin, was it?' enquired Lady Margrave.

'It was actually,' answered Marie.

'He seems like a nice man, with a great career before him. But, a little staid in his ways I think.'

Marie smiled, Lady Margrave was

absolutely right. There was something stiff and formal about Sam, which made him seem older than his years. She suspected it came partly from his profession, where a poker face and an ability to hide your emotions was a useful attribute.

When Lady Margrave went up for her nap that afternoon, Marie was poring over the accounts book with a pile of household bills in front of her. A house as large as Margrave Manor was quite complicated in its upkeep so Marie had made files for each of the utilities so that the invoices, which had been in one unruly pile, could be kept tidily in order. As she sat at the desk, there was a tap at the French windows.

There, with a streak of mud down his face and looking rakish in jeans and a jeans shirt, stood Matthew, with his hand held behind his back. When she opened the door, he bowed, brought his hand forward and there, was the most delightful bunch of twelve *Deep Secret* roses.

'Milady' he announced, his head still deeply bowed, his chin almost touching his knee. Tied with a piece of gardener's string, they were no less beautiful for being simply presented.

'You may arise now, Sir Matthew,' joked Marie.

After they laughed at the impromptu play-acting, there was a nervous silence. 'You said these are your favourite so I picked them for you. I have to keep picking the standard roses or they get top heavy and topple in the wind.' Matthew was speaking so quickly, Marie detected the nervousness he felt at offering them to her. 'You do like them, don't you?'

'They're gorgeous,' she said taking them and breathing in their rich sweet scent. 'I shall put them here on the desk, Lady Margrave likes them too.'

'No, don't do that,' Matthew's dark expressive eyes pleaded, 'I've done Lady M a bunch of gladioli for in here. Those are yours. For your room.'

Marie had never been given roses

before, let alone ones as fine as this. They were ten times nicer than florists' roses with their lanky stems and lack of scent. These were real, full blooded and exotic.

'Must dash now,' he said and strode off across the lawn. Marie cradled the roses in her arm and watched his fine figure retreating, before she went off to find a vase. If she could have one wish granted at that moment, it would be that Matthew Hughes would not turn out to be the person stealing from Lady Margrave.

The next day Marie and Lady Margrave set to archiving some old files and throwing out papers from years ago.

'Here is a book with the names and addresses of all the staff who've ever worked at Margrave Manor. I've sometimes thought of throwing it out, it's of no real use. But then I do still sometimes get asked for references if people go abroad and then come back to work in the UK. What do you think,

Marie, should we keep it?'

Marie leafed through the book; flattered that Lady Margrave should be seeking her opinion so early on in her service at Margrave Manor.

'It's fascinating, look at all these maids and parlour maids. I think you should keep it, if nothing else as an interesting piece of social history. Look at these lovely names, Maisie Pike, Tilly Burrows you can imagine them in their little black dresses and white pinnies.'

'You're right, let's keep it. What's more, we'll add you in as well, with your last known address. There, now it's properly up to date. We've thrown out a lot of other stuff today so I feel quite virtuous.'

Lady Margrave pushed the book back in the drawer it had come from and sat looking tired but satisfied in her easy chair. 'How did your trip into the town go? I heard you come in, did someone give you a lift back?'

'Yes, it was Sam Martin. I bumped into him at the police station and he introduced me to some of the locals. Lady Margrave?' Marie asked as she tied up the black rubbish sack with all the old papers. 'Have you met Mrs Johnson's daughter, Sadie?'

'I have had that dubious pleasure.'

'Oh dear.' Marie wondered what she should read into that comment but Lady Margrave hastened to explain, as soon as she'd said it.

'I don't want to be unkind. I know that Sadie is a bubbly, fun-loving girl. But, as soon as she hit her teens she was going out with boys and I think has matured a lot faster than she ought to have done. A friend of mine was looking out for help with some cleaning and general household duties and Mrs Johnson was keen for Sadie to take on the role. But her daughter wasn't interested. Sadie, I think, is a girl who is constantly on the look out for the next amusement.' Marie could believe that, but she thought no more about Sadie that day, being too busy with other things.

As Marie lugged the big rubbish bag out to the back door, she found Mrs Johnson sitting at the kitchen table, a cup of cold tea in front of her. Gyp sat at her feet, looking up at her wide eyed. 'Are you OK, Mrs Johnson?'

It struck Marie how unusual it was to see the housekeeper unoccupied. Mrs Johnson may not have been terribly warm towards her but she was a good hard-working woman. It was unusual to see her so far away in thought and in particular with such a worried expression on her face.

'I'm fine,' Mrs Johnson shook herself out of her reverie. 'I just have lots of things on my mind at present. You'll know if you ever have children how worrying they are, even when they're grown up.' So saying, she picked up her cup and started washing it vigorously.

All that left Marie's mind when she jumped in the car with Sam Martin to go off to the concert. For some reason Marie couldn't understand, she didn't want Matthew to see her going out with Sam.

It wasn't as if she was going out as in girlfriend and boyfriend with either Matthew or Sam. But, she rather liked the company of both of them, as friends. Matthew's kiss, and his gift of roses she believed was born more out of his natural exuberance than anything else. That was the way he was. That was what made him attractive but she felt, she might get very hurt if she read anything more into it.

Sam and Matthew were like chalk and cheese she thought as she sat next to a silent Sam as he expertly navigated the car down the country lanes. There was no real indication that either of them was interested in her particularly and besides, the memory of Adrian was too fresh in her consciousness for her to want a relationship at the moment. A new job with all the challenges that brought was more than enough to keep her busy.

The concert was held in a big church

an hour's drive away, where a pair of classical guitarists played a varied programme of set pieces. The repertoire included light and summery South American songs and intricate works by Bach. Marie found herself transported by the music and was very grateful to Sam for bringing her.

During the intermission they stood drinking a glass of wine and nibbling crisps in the crowded crypt. Marie had worn a black short-sleeved dress, with a white pashmina to keep her shoulders warm. As it slid off, Sam leaned over and rearranged it on her shoulders. Just as they were involved in this intimate moment, a blonde woman a little older than Marie walked past with her partner and suddenly exclaimed, 'Sam, I thought it was you. Where's Naomi?'

'Hello, Sarah,' he quickly dropped his hand from Marie's shoulder and she thought he looked uncomfortably surprised. 'How are you?'

'I'm fine. Isn't it a wonderful concert?'

'Yes, very fine playing.' Sam's voice was even more clipped than usual as he continued. 'I think we'd better get back. They're about to start the second half.'

'Of course, goodbye.' The young woman watched them go.

Marie thought she detected a puzzled look on the girl's face and when they had sat down and were waiting for the musicians to re-take their seats, she said in her direct way, 'Who's Naomi.'

6

Sam turned a bright smile on her and said, 'She's my ex. I haven't seen Sarah in ages and she obviously thought Naomi and I were still together. But, it's been over more than a year now.'

'Right,' answered Marie thinking back to Adrian. Any mention of him made her feel nervous. So, that explained why Sam had looked a little uneasy. He obviously wouldn't want to talk about a failed relationship when he was trying to forget it. She settled down to listen to the second half.

As soon as the concert was over, Sam seemed to want to rush her away; 'if we hurry, there's time enough for a drink at a nice little pub I know on the way back.'

The pub was very olde worlde with horse brasses hanging from the walls, low ceilings and funny rickety old floors which were so uneven they almost made you feel as if you were on board a ship. While they were drinking, Sam told Marie all the things he was doing to investigate the thefts at Margrave Manor.

'There haven't been any leads so far although I've made sure the patrol cars vary their routes slightly so that they drive past more often, particularly at night. That prowler must have been significant and we can only hope that having got away with it twice, he tries again.'

'I must admit,' said Marie, a shiver running down her spine, 'that the thought of someone breaking in, perhaps when we're asleep is very unsettling.'

'It is indeed although something tells me this isn't a normal run of the mill burglary simply because if it was, the burglar would have to have left signs of breaking in. There would be a forced lock or broken glass somewhere. I have a strong feeling it is someone who has a key. We've dusted for fingerprints, but all the ones we found match people who are known to have business at the Manor. I don't think you have anything to fear; all the burglar wanted is the goods so that he or she can make a quick sale.'

'The fact that they are stealing things one by one means that they are looking on Margrave Manor as a steady stream of income and they don't want to kill the goose that lays the golden egg by doing anything rash. They certainly don't want a stash of goods in their house. They just want to steal individual items and shift them as quickly as possible.'

Marie looked troubled as she toyed with one of the beer mats. 'I discussed with Lady Margrave the other day fitting a burglar alarm but she wasn't keen. She said she would feel as if she was under siege if she did that and she doesn't trust the new technology. She said a friend of hers who has one is always having it go off by mistake and that they're difficult if you have pets who can set them off. Besides, she thinks that dear old Gyp will save any of us if there were someone who tried to attack.'

'I think she's right there. He's a loyal dog and well behaved. But of course, that's another part of the mystery.'

'What do you mean?'

'It must be someone Gyp knows. I know he isn't a yappy dog, but if someone came into the house who he didn't know I'm sure he'd raise the alarm. When I called that first day with my assistant, he growled and I'm sure he would have been ready to attack if it weren't for the fact that Lady Margrave stroked him and calmed him down.'

'I've been having my people go around the area asking questions and keeping an eye on the auction rooms as well. We'll crack it, given time.'

There was something very reassuring about Sam's cool, measured approach, which summed him up generally. As he pulled into the driveway a little later and turned the ignition off in the car he said, 'I'll walk you to the front door.'

'Really, it's not necessary.' Marie picked her way carefully over the gravel in her kitten heels.

'I insist,' said Sam kindly.

'Well,' whispered Marie on the doorstep, 'it's been a lovely evening I did enjoy the concert. Thank you so much.'

'Thank you for accompanying me. I haven't said yet how pretty you looked tonight.'

Marie put her head down and muttered a brief embarrassed 'thank you.' When she looked up, Sam had moved a little closer and for a second, she had the feeling he was going to kiss her.

'Goodbye Sam,' she said shyly and gently shut the door.

★　★　★

The garden-opening fund-raiser was booked for the following day. For the

101

last few days, Marie had sprung out of bed in the morning and studied the sky. It had thankfully been relentlessly cornflower blue with not a cloud in sight. It was even warming up and becoming muggy.

From what people had said to her in the pub where she'd distributed leaflets, Marie calculated that they would have at least one hundred people visiting.

She and Matthew had got together some old trestle tables that were languishing in a shed and had set them up at the far end of the lawn. They laid out hundreds of healthy-potted cuttings and labelled them carefully with the name and the price so that it all looked very professional.

Marie pulled down and clicked into place the legs on one of the trestles. 'We can't possibly do all the setting up on the morning of the opening as we're letting people in as early as possible, so we need to get as many things in place as early as possible.'

'You've got everything planned out

haven't you, Marie. I've been thinking it through myself too. Let's lay up the round tables near the lake with the fold-up chairs, and I'll put up the small marquee. That can be for Mrs Johnson's cakes. There's power in the greenhouse and it's only a short walk away so we can set up the tea urn you've hired and it will be like a proper professional event. At least if the marquee is there, we'll be covered, literally, whether it's sunny or rainy.'

'Don't mention rain, Matthew, or you'll be tempting the gods. I couldn't bear it if we had rain. All this depends on our so-called Indian Summer continuing.'

'It's been gorgeous weather so far, I'm sure it will hold.'

The two of them worked all day, carrying plants back and forth, wheeling chairs into place and setting up the marquee until Marie's feet were burning and her back twinged. But she was so excited about the target she had set for them to achieve; she really thought they could raise enough to buy a whole library for the school in India.

Later in the day, Lady Margrave came out to view all the arrangements, together with Mrs Johnson. 'And this is where people will sit to have their tea and coffee and eat tons of your wonderful cake, Mrs Johnson.'

Mrs Johnson smiled and said, 'I hope they do eat tons, because tons is what I've got. The freezer's near to bursting. I'm going to take them all out tonight and line them up around the kitchen to defrost. We can bring them down to this marquee first thing in the morning.'

Lady Margrave cast an approving eye over what looked like a traditional garden party. 'It really does look perfect, you two have created a lovely setting here by the lake. And it's so incredibly muggy today. If it's like this tomorrow, by the lake will be the only cool place to be. Now, I want to do as much as I can to help. Just because I'm older than you young things doesn't mean I can't be useful.'

'If it's all right with you, Lady Margrave,' Marie consulted her notes; 'I've put you on door duty. You'll be at the front gate selling tickets and meeting and greeting people. I think the first thing they'll want to do is meet the Lady of the Manor.'

'That sounds excellent. I've managed to get a couple of my friends along from the Bridge Club, Elaine and Margaret, so we'll help in relays.'

'Terrific,' Marie felt she was riding on the crest of the wave; everything seemed to be going so well. 'I've bought in loads of packets of tea and coffee, and the milkman is delivering two crates of milk. I just hope it all goes to plan and all that milk gets drunk.'

'Your plans always seem to work out,' said Matthew encouragingly, flashing her a grin. Marie's heart warmed to him, he had the same drive and positive outlook she had. She would never have got this project off the ground without him.

'If it's all right with you, Mrs

Johnson, you will man the tea tent.'

'Sounds fine,' responded Mrs Johnson briskly. 'I've always fancied opening a tea room and now I'll be able to give it a go.'

★　★　★

Marie crashed into bed that night exhausted and hardly able to drop off to sleep, her head was so full of the arrangements for the next day. Lying in her bed, as soon as her mind began to shut off, another thought buzzed into it. Did she have enough paper cups, had she bought in sugar? Finally, thankfully, she dropped off. She was woken however in the middle of the night feeling incredibly hot and hearing a rumbling sound which woke her with a start, realising what she'd heard had been thunder.

She rushed over to the window and prayed it was not going to rain. But then, big fat drops started to descend through the thickly warm air. Just a few at first, then a torrent was unleashed. Marie's spirits crashed to rock bottom. Why now, of all nights? This was a disaster. Sheets of unbroken heavy rain lashed at the window. A clap of thunder shook the windows, making Marie jump. Wind tore at the trees, and angry lightening flashed across the sky.

As it illuminated the garden, Marie felt like crying. All she could see was rain running like rivers along the paths and spilling off the patio. In utter, abject misery, she took to her bed convinced that tomorrow was going to be a complete unmitigated disaster and drifted off into a miserable fitful sleep.

The next morning she was almost scared to get out of bed and look out to see what damage the storm had wreaked. She lay like a statue and listened to see if it were still raining. No-one would turn up if it were. Who on earth would want to tramp over sodden lawns looking at plants, which had been beaten down by the storm? She swung her legs heavily over the side of the bed and decided she could delay no longer.

But, as she drew the curtains, brilliant sunshine greeted her. She crinkled her eyes to look in the distance and noticed gentle eddies of steam over the lake being swirled by the whisper of a breeze. Opening the window, all the close mugginess of the day before had disappeared and been replaced by refreshing brightness. Azure blue skies seemed to spread forever and a couple of early morning butterflies danced above a cluster of pink nerines. It was perfect, utterly, sublimely perfect.

With a spring in her step, Marie rushed down the passage to get washed and ready. Lady Margrave and her friends were in their element, wearing large floppy hats against the sparkling sun, they gave everyone copies of the carefully thought out garden plan which Marie had produced and chatted to people making them feel welcome as they took their entrance fees.

Mrs Johnston started delivering teas

and coffees from the large silver urn the minute the gates opened and after only an hour, had to empty her tin of silver into Marie's cash box to make way for more takings.

Matthew was charm itself, giving cultural instructions to people who bought plants and at one stage, standing with such a group of customers around him that he was like a lecturer giving a talk. His easy affable manner and funny jokes had people telling him he should be on television, one woman even pronouncing him to be 'better than all those so-called TV gardeners who are full of themselves and don't tell you enough about the plants.'

The takings on the plant stall manned by Marie and Matthew were particularly high and Marie had quite a bundle of notes gathered in the cash box under the plant table. She kept a close eye on it.

Once the morning was over they had so much, she needed to go back inside the house and lock the box in Lady Margrave's morning room. She had just enough time to count the notes, it was an extremely respectable amount already!

She didn't have enough time to count the coins but the box was very heavy, so it should well exceed her expectations. She put the full box in the desk drawer and grabbed the empty reserve cash box she had put aside. Hurrying back out into the garden, she carefully locked the French doors behind her.

As she arrived at the plant stall it seemed, for the first time in the day, to be quiet. 'We're running out of plants, I've sold loads,' stated Matthew with pride. 'I've got just half a dozen more boxes we could sell if you want to. I'd been keeping those back to replenish the garden next year but quite frankly if this good weather is going to last, I can take some more cuttings and raise some from seed to fill up our borders. If you're happy, we could get the boxes from the greenhouse now.'

'Absolutely,' breezed Marie, 'the

more the merrier.'

As they stood in the greenhouse and placed all the plants in the boxes, Matthew turned to her and said, 'I'm really enjoying today. It was a brilliant idea of yours. So many people have come up to compliment me on my work, it's been a real tonic.'

'Thank you,' beamed Marie.

Impulsively, Matthew took her in a hug and said, 'you've really shaken us out of ourselves, it was the best day when you arrived at Margrave Manor.'

Marie was glowing inside until she heard a deep, low voice behind them say, 'ahem.' Marie whirled around and Matthew released her to see Sam Martin standing at the door. His face was like a blank emotionless canvas, 'if you have a moment, Miss Clarke,' he said formally, 'I'd like a word.'

'Of course,' Marie brushed herself down.

'I can carry the plants through on my own, Marie, don't worry,' said Matthew throwing Sam a look and striding out of the greenhouse.

Marie accompanied Sam to one of the quieter parts of the garden. His face was as immovable as a mask, impossible to read, but it was obvious he had seen her and Matthew together and seemed particularly cold about it. Could it be that he, like Mrs Johnson was judging Matthew by the errors he had made in his youth, rather than the person he was today? But then again, perhaps they were better judges of character than she was.

Marie felt as if her emotions were being tossed on a very stormy sea. 'I thought you ought to know, Marie, that the figurine of the dog has turned up in an auction room on the other side of the county.'

7

Marie gasped. She couldn't believe that things were moving so swiftly. 'Does that mean you've found the thief?'

'It's not as easy as that. The dealer who put it in the sale was sold it by another dealer who bought if off a man for cash. The only trouble is, he was having a busy day at his antiques shop and has given us such a general description of the man who sold it to him, it's worse than useless. He had a large coach party of Americans descend on his shop at the same time and was inundated with business. He barely noticed the man who sold him the figurine. One thing it does mean though . . . '

'What?'

'Our man or woman probably lives not far from here.'

A cloud descended over Marie's face

as she put two and two together. But, she didn't need to put her concerns into words, as Sam did that for her. 'I take it Matthew Hughes is still living in the cottage on this estate.'

Marie's eyes dropped. 'Yes, of course he is.'

'Thank you, Marie, you've been very helpful.'

'One more thing?' she asked.

'Yes.'

'Do you think we can assume that because the person who sold the figurine is a man, that the thief is a man?'

'You can never make assumptions in this game. Thieves often work with accomplices. What we need now are some hard facts. I'll let you get on with your fund-raiser I've seen a couple of people here from the police station, they're all very impressed with your efforts.'

'Thank you, Sam. I hope you have time to look around.'

'I'll have to do that another time,' his

voice was coldly businesslike. 'I have things I must attend to now.'

Later in the day, once most of the plants had been sold, Marie went to give Lady Margrave a hand at the entrance. People were still filtering through, and Lady Margrave's two friends had gone home, only able to help out in the morning. Marie could see the old lady was overjoyed with the response, but exhausted with all the activity and the heat.

'I really feel quite woozy, my dear. I'm getting a bit confused now with all this money and tickets and things because I'm so tired. I would have liked to sit here the whole day but I have to admit that I can't cope with any more, without having my afternoon nap.'

'Goodness,' uttered Marie. 'I'm so sorry, in all the excitement I forgot you haven't had a rest all day.' She handed Lady Margrave her walking stick and watched as Lady Margrave picked up the biscuit tin with the takings. 'There's too much change in there to fit in any more money. There's an empty tin there for you, Marie, which should be big enough to collect the money from the last few people who may come through.'

'I'll be fine,' said Marie, then, seeing Lady Margrave stumble slightly she jumped up and said, 'here, let me help you inside, I'm keeping all the money locked in the morning room. It won't take a minute and I can't see any people coming up the road.'

As she took Lady Margrave's arm, she saw the old lady's eyelids looking droopy. Marie left her at the door to the morning room as Lady Margrave commanded, 'You go back and man that gate. I'll just lock the tin away in here and then go up for a nap. Go on, away with you, I don't need any more help. I can cope.'

Smiling at her fierce independence, Marie went back to the table and chair at the front gate just in time to issue tickets to a family of four. By 6 p.m. it was all over.

As she was folding the table and chairs up by the front gate and preparing to take them back to the shed, Mrs Johnson came up to her, holding her tin of money. She rattled it and said, 'Every single slice of my cakes was sold. In fact, I believe I could have sold more if I'd baked more but there's only so much one woman can do on her own.'

'You've done fantastically well, Mrs Johnson. Refreshments are such a wonderful way to make extra funds because you can put a huge mark up on them.'

'You're right there, I'd never thought people would pay what we were charging for one slice of cake. We've made a terrific profit on each one. I have to hand it to you, Marie Clarke, you've got a good business brain on you.'

Coming from the brittle Mrs Johnson that was praise indeed. 'I wish the same could be said for my Sadie. She's looking for work, yet again.'

'I'm sure she'll find something soon, Mrs Johnson, young people are always in demand, they have such energy.'

'Hmm well, whether they have energy and whether they choose to use it are two different things. She could easily get a job cleaning or waiting at tables but she seems to think she's either too good for that, or that she can find some man to support her. Anyway, I can't be standing here chatting to you all day. I presume you're keeping all the takings in the office in the morning room. I'll drop this tin in there and go and clear up my poor old kitchen.'

Gyp who had spent most of the day trying to keep cool in Mrs Johnson's cake tent wandered after her with his tail wagging.

By the time they had cleared up all the tables and chairs, gone around and picked up all the stray serviettes and leaflets that people had dropped in the garden, it was dark. Marie was shattered.

'You need an early night, you look all

in,' said Matthew, concern clouding his bright, observant eyes.

'I'll try and get my head down as soon as possible, but before I do, I need to go and count all that money. I'm desperate to know how much we made, and I'd also like to get it banked tomorrow so it's not lying around.'

'I'd give you a hand, but it's my day off tomorrow. I'm off to a car auction in Wadsham, so I need to make an early start.'

'Are you buying or selling?'

'No-one would buy my old wreck, although I might make a bit on it for scrap. No, I'm mainly looking to buy. Something a bit more up market. I've told Mrs Johnson I'll take Gyp. The auction's held in a big field and he likes a good old run around. Besides he's company for me on the drive.'

Matthew didn't see the troubled look on Marie's face as she made her way back into the house. She didn't want to think unkind thoughts about Matthew, but when they'd had their dinner together the other night, he'd told her how he had to do all the repairs and maintenance on the cottage himself because he didn't have enough money to call people in.

He said that Lady Margrave had let him live in the property for a very low rent on the understanding that he would maintain it. Where on earth was Matthew going to get the money for a new car, even if it was second hand?

When she got into the morning room she recalled that she hadn't seen Lady Margrave for the rest of the day. She must have needed some peace and quiet, and had probably gone to bed early.

Yawning, but forcing herself to sit down and count the takings, Marie first of all spilled the collection of coins and notes from Mrs Johnson's tin on to the desk, carefully counted it all up, sorted it into bank paying in bags and entered it into an accounts book.

Then she counted the door takings, which was all in coins. She then unlocked the cash box for the plant sales. As she lifted the lid, something struck her immediately. Where was the roll of notes? Marie suddenly felt her heart shoot into her throat. She scrabbled to lift the inner tray, but there were only coins underneath.

Marie felt a horrible gripping pain in her stomach. Where had all that money gone? They had taken far, far more than was here. At least three quarters had disappeared. Some people had bought bagfuls of plants, and Marie distinctly remembered seeing a handful of £20 notes when she had counted the bundle earlier. Loads of the money was missing.

In desperation, her knees weak, Marie got up to see if by any chance they had somehow fallen out of the cash tin and were perhaps in a bundle on the carpet somewhere. But, she knew she was clutching at straws. She searched under the desk, under tables and chairs. They had gone. A large amount of takings of the plant stall had simply disappeared.

Feeling nauseous, Marie meticulously counted up what takings there were, put them into bank bags and made a note of them. She then put the whole lot into an envelope and into the safe.

Had someone taken the money? She, Mrs Johnson, Matthew and Lady Margrave all had access to the morning room. The key was always kept in the same secret place.

If only, thought Marie, anxiety wrinkling her brow, if only she had taken the time to put the money straight in the safe which only she and Lady Margrave had the combination to. If only she'd kept the money on her. But, as the old saying goes, 'if ifs and ands were pots and pans, there'd be no work for tinkers.' She couldn't turn back the clock. She would have to burden Lady Margrave with the fact that a substantial amount of the money had disappeared but she would let her employer sleep now and give her the bad news tomorrow.

The next day, Lady Margrave was still in her bedroom mid-morning, which was most unlike her. As Marie sat in the morning room, doing her work and steeling herself to break the bad news to Lady Margrave, Mrs Johnson knocked on the door.

'I've been up to see Lady Margrave and she's taken a turn for the worse. She seems to have some kind of flu, poor thing, she's coughing and head-achy.'

'Oh, no,' said Marie with feeling. 'Is there anything I can do?'

'Well, if you're going into town, perhaps you'd pick up some medicine, some orange juice and a few other things. I'll give you a list.'

Armed with the list, Marie went first to bank the money that they had taken, and then on to the shops. On her way back, she encountered Sam Martin who asked her how she was and offered to take her for a coffee. She felt in need of a pick-me-up and was pleased that, after his coldness yesterday, Sam seemed a bit more friendly today. 'We could go to the coffee shop on the high street, I've just passed it and they're not busy,' she said.

'We're better off at the coffee shop on the edge of town,' said Sam, 'I can give you a lift there and then drop you off back at the Manor.'

'OK then,' said Marie. It made no difference to her, but she wondered why they didn't just go to the nearest coffee shop which she'd found clean and friendly on the few occasions she'd used it. This one was much quieter and more out of the way. There were seats near the window, which she generally preferred, but Sam led her to the back, which was a little darker.

'Can I get you a cake or something with your coffee?'

'Why not?' said Marie. 'I didn't have any breakfast so I could do with one.'

While waiting for their order, Marie suddenly jumped and let out a squeal, as a spider ran across the floor. 'I don't know why you're making such a fuss,' said Sam, somewhat tersely. 'It's only a spider. You must expect those now that you're out in the country a bit and no longer in the city.'

Marie felt a little crestfallen but didn't show it. His voice had been harsher than she'd ever heard it. 'Sorry, Sam.'

'It's just that I've always had a bit of a phobia about spiders. My mother did and I suppose she's passed it on to me. I know it's silly of me.'

'Forget it,' said Sam resting his hand over hers on the table. 'I'm sorry, Marie. And I'm sorry I was a bit short with you yesterday at the fund-raiser. It's just that you seemed to be having such a nice time with Matthew Hughes and there I was having to work on various cases, none of which I'm afraid are coming together. I'd have much rather been spending time with you. I guess I was a bit jealous.'

'Jealous?' Marie said in amazement. She'd never had anyone jealous over her, especially not someone so nice looking and level headed as Sam.

'I can see I've embarrassed you now.' He smiled. He had a nice smile but, as always, guarded. She couldn't imagine Sam betraying his emotions in anything like the way Matthew Hughes did. When the waitress came with their order, Marie removed her hand from underneath Sam's and put it back in her lap as the tray was laid down on the table.

If the truth were told, he unsettled her a bit. One minute he was nice to her, the next he seemed so gruff. 'Well, I'm gong to embarrass you a bit more. The thing is, Marie, you have no idea how pretty you are, do you?'

Marie felt two hot pink spots appear on her cheeks. All she could do was mutter, 'thank you.' It wasn't the sort of thing she was used to at all. To change the subject she said, 'Have you got any more news about the thefts?'

'No,' he sat back in his chair. 'I suppose that's one of the reasons why

I'm a bit on edge. I'm drawing blanks wherever I look, but there'll be a breakthrough soon, I know there will.'

It crossed her mind to tell him about the missing money, but Marie decided for some reason to wait for a while. She still hoped the money might turn up, because if it didn't, it meant that surely the eye of suspicion would fall on Matthew.

If Matthew had stolen it, then he ought to face up to the music but for now and certainly until she could speak to Lady Margrave, Marie chose not to tell Sam about it. Marie thanked him for coffee and for the lift back to the house.

When she got back to the Manor, Mrs Johnson said that Lady Margrave was still in bed and had asked not to be disturbed. Marie carried on with her work and then, in the evening went up to her bedroom to read. Later on, she became restless and decided to take herself out for a short walk.

The evening was fine and, wrapping

up in a warm jacket and putting flat shoes on, she went down into the hall. There was Gyp, laying down looking tired. Marie remembered that Matthew had taken him to the auction and that Gyp would have had a good run around the field where the cars were displayed. Gyp certainly didn't show any signs of wanting a walk now, so she left him there.

Letting herself out of the door, Marie decided to follow the footpath, which ran off into the woods near Matthew's cottage. At this time of year it was lined with blackberries and shiny red rose-hips. To get to the cottage she had to walk up part of Matthew's driveway. As she did, she saw, to her amazement that the old car he had was gone. In its place stood a much newer black car.

So, he had managed to buy a new car. Marie pulled her jacket about her, feeling herself shiver. Where on earth had the money come for that? Walking on, into the woods and across a nearby field, she had more on her mind than she wanted. When she came back, it was almost dark. She found that physical activity always made her feel better and, although she didn't have any solutions to all the conundrums which were flying about in her head, at least she felt the exercise might help her get to sleep.

Making her way back, the way she had come, Marie almost collided with a small slim figure wearing a coat with a hood on. 'Oh, sorry,' said Marie. As the figure looked up and muttered a quick sorry, Marie realised it was Sadie Johnson. And this time, she wasn't coming away from Margrave Manor; she was coming directly from Matthew Hughes's cottage. In a complete fluster, Marie hurried off and ran back to the Manor house.

A black empty feeling fell over Marie as she shot upstairs and sat panting on her bed. How could he? Matthew was obviously seeing Sadie otherwise why would she be there at this time of the evening. If the two of them were an item, how could he possibly have kissed Marie the other day, told her how nice she looked, entertained her to dinner at his cottage? She had never been two timed before and she most certainly didn't want to be now.

Although Marie wasn't going out with Matthew he'd certainly flirted with her. He'd shown her he was interested and been very tactile with her in a manner that led her to believe there might at some point be something more intimate between them.

When it came down to it, the reason Marie felt so shocked by seeing Sadie Johnson coming away from Matthew's cottage was that she realised she was falling in love with him.

The knowledge hit her like a truck at full speed. How could he? She thought again. It was cruel. She thought back to what Mrs Johnson had said about him not being all he seemed to be. Well that was certainly true. If he could be duplicitous, seeing someone behind her back, maybe he had lied and had taken the figurine, the painting and finally the money.

Curling up in bed, Marie felt a bitterness grip her heart. She had been so right initially to think that after breaking up with Adrian she didn't want another relationship for a very long time. Relationships were nothing but trouble. They lead to misery and hurt and empty, cavernous nights like this. As Marie lay longing for the oblivion of sleep, dark, soul-wrenching thoughts crowded her head.

8

The next day, Marie resolved to try and be professional and concentrate on her work. That is what she had come here to do, and that must be her main priority. There was a pile of correspondence that had come in for Lady Margrave but Marie didn't want to trouble her with it. Marie instead sorted through everything, spoke to some people on the phone to tell them that they would receive slightly belated replies and, drafted responses so that when Lady Margrave was better, she could simply sign them off or revise them where necessary.

All this activity did help a little to divert her from the upset of the previous day although every now and then it came back to haunt her. When she heard a tap at the window and saw Matthew standing outside, looking very purposeful, frankly Marie did not want to talk to him. As he was insistent, she opened the door and was met with his usual bright, 'How are you?'

'Not bad.' Marie was aware that her voice was curt and flat.

'Are you OK, you don't sound too good?' he asked with one eyebrow raised. Marie didn't want him caring about her. After all, he presumably had Sadie Johnson to care about. It didn't help that he looked particularly appealing today, his hair tousled and boyish as if he had been running his fingers through it. His eyes were full of concern.

'Marie, you don't look too good. Have you not been sleeping well? You must take care of yourself. You don't want to go down with Lady Margrave's cold, she relies on you too much. We all do.'

'Hmm,' was the only answer Marie gave to that? 'Did you want something?'

Still looking troubled at her reaction, he now spoke with a more serious look on his face than it ever usually held. 'I wondered if you had the phone number for that Detective Sergeant Martin. I've just had a thought about something a bit odd I wanted to mention to him.'

'Really?' Marie didn't feel like giving him more than a one-word answer. She scribbled the number down on a piece of paper and handed it to him. 'I'm afraid I have to get back to my work now.' She said a brisk goodbye and closed the French doors. Her heart felt heavy and sad as she watched him walk away, shoulders low. Unexpectedly, he looked back and as his gaze settled on her, she turned her back on him and put her head down to concentrate on her work.

Later in the day, Marie went up to see Lady Margrave. The poor old lady looked washed out, but she was at least sitting up in bed. 'I've been very poorly, my dear, hardly able to keep my eyes open,' Lady Margrave's voice was still hoarse and gravelly. 'And you wouldn't believe what a sore throat I had.'

'Are you feeling a little better now?'

'Yes, a lot better thank you. Mrs Johnson has been very good. She's a little strict as a nurse, but she kept me well supplied with hot toddies and throat lozenges. I worry about her sometimes; she really has her hands full at the moment with that dreadful daughter of hers. She was chattering to me about her. I think she wanted to take my mind off how unwell I was feeling, and bring the outside world in to divert me a little.'

'It's very good of you to worry about others when you've been so unwell yourself.'

'Oh tosh, I'm interested in people, I always have been. I'll let you into a little secret; I've always been a bit nosey. People intrigue me. I guess I like my own little soap operas which go on around me. You'll find they're always present when you run a big household like this. Mrs Johnson's daughter, Sadie, is like a soap opera herself. She gets the most awful crushes on men, pursues them like the little minx she is and then the next week has latched on to some other poor hapless male.'

'Well, it's good to see you sitting up and smiling again. I feel terribly guilty, wondering if it was the fund-raiser and all that hard work that had made you ill.'

'Absolutely not. I was feeling a tad throaty the day before but I didn't want to tell anyone. After all, I had to do my bit, didn't I? I have been dying to know anyway, how much did we make?'

Marie went to speak but couldn't find the right words. She had so wanted this moment to be a triumphant announcement of what they had raised and yet it was tinged with difficulty because of the theft. She told Lady Margrave the amount that had been raised but then swiftly said, 'but I'm afraid some of the money has gone missing as well.'

'Missing?' Lady Margrave sat bolt upright.

'Yes,' Marie went on to relate that the

bundle of notes had disappeared.

'That is scandalous, how could anyone steal money knowing it was for a charitable cause. To deny all those little children in India their rightful money when we here are all so comfortable in comparison. Such greed is abhorrent.' Marie couldn't have agreed more.

'But what should we do about it? I've been in a terrible quandary and hardly able to sleep. But, you are head of the household and although I know that the police would be the natural people to tell, I wanted to speak to you first because . . . well, because . . . '

Lady Margrave leant forward and took Marie's face between her bony hands. 'You don't have to say what is troubling you, my dear, because I know exactly what implications this has. You and I both know that we, and Mrs Johnson and Matthew Hughes were the only four people who had access to the key. It narrows the field right down for suspects for the thefts, doesn't it? We now know it has to have been one of us four people. Someone in my household is stealing from me, that is for certain.' Lady Margrave let her hands drop tiredly by her side.

Marie felt tears prick the back of her eyes. She had become so happy here but she had to admit that the conclusion Lady Margrave had come to was one which she herself had mulled over again and again in her mind and it was impossible to deny.

Marie felt her hand begin to shake, it was all so horrible. She knew she hadn't stolen anything and yet if people found out about her father's gambling debts they may feel that someone from a dishonest family was in their midst and put two and two together to make five.

Although Sam Martin had said that prowlers had been seen around the Manor before Marie's arrival it now seemed a major coincidence that all the thefts had taken place since she arrived.

Mrs Johnson, although prickly, had seemed an upright and honest woman with many years service, but then again her daughter was acknowledged to be the sort of girl whom trouble followed like a bad and wayward companion. Had Sadie got herself into some sort of financial trouble where she needed ready money? Maybe the argument that she and Mrs Johnson had had the other night was something to do with that.

Matthew Hughes had seemed so kind and so much fun but that could all be a veneer hiding someone who would steal from a kind employer. It made Marie shudder to think how she had been falling for his easy charm. And what had Sadie Johnson been doing coming away from his cottage so late? Marie couldn't help herself, she put her face in her hands in a gesture of despair.

'There, there, my dear, don't look like that. Somehow, we shall get to the bottom of this. I still feel weak, but I am determined to get up today and go downstairs. It doesn't do to be lying around. I feel that when my mind is not active, I am easily confused and fall into a sort of fog. Lying up here, barely knowing what time of day it is has not been good for me. I want you to go downstairs and get some work ready for me. I shall be down after lunch and we shall engage our minds on something worthwhile and positive.'

Marie smiled at the older woman. 'You're so wise, Lady Margrave. I'll go and get some things ready right now.'

'That's the spirit, inactivity is bad for the soul as well as the body you know.'

They spent a pleasant afternoon working through the papers and letters and although Lady Margrave still wasn't one hundred percent, getting back on her feet seemed to make her feel a lot better.

As the afternoon was getting on, they heard a scuffling and a tapping at the morning room door. Marie opened it to find Gyp sitting there patiently. 'Are you wanting to go for a walk, boy?' she asked. 'We've still got more work to do, I'm afraid.'

'Actually, I think I've done what I

can today. I think I should be easing myself back to work slowly. Why don't you take Gyp out for a good long run, it's a lovely afternoon and I'm sure you'd enjoy the exercise.'

Marie stretched her arms and felt the tension in her shoulders. 'You're right, I would like to get out for a bit. What about those files, let me put those away first.'

'No, I insist,' Lady Margrave waved her off. 'I can put these away, a little bit of stretching won't do me any harm. Off with you now, I'm not infirm yet you know.'

Marie gratefully took the keys from the hook, grabbed a cardigan and let the overjoyed Gyp out, wagging his tail wildly and jumping up and down. The afternoon was warm and sunny with a pleasant breeze.

Marie strode out, trying to clear her mind of all that had been going on. Gyp scuttled along the well-worn footpaths on the circuit that they always took. It was a while since she had taken him for a long run, and he was excited all the way.

She walked down the stony path with the long grass of a fallow field on one side, its wild flowers having gone to seed. On the other were the blunt spiky straws of a field that had been cropped and harvested. Marie breathed in, filling her lungs with the scent of newly-cut hay.

After about twenty minutes, Marie decided it was time to turn back, but Gyp had other ideas. 'Here Gyp, here Gyp, come on.' Marie started to get worried about him as they were near the road and she always tried to move on as quickly as possible from this spot.

He was a good dog, and usually whenever he got near a road, he would wait patiently for her. She started to run up the footpath and then suddenly, the sickening sound of grating brakes and a screech came to her ears.

'Gyp, Gyp,' she cried out. As she got to the road, she saw a car with a young woman in it, stopped near the hedge-erow, with its door wide open and the woman looking helplessly down. There was poor Gyp, lying on the ground unconscious, his leg bloodied.

'Oh no,' said the woman leaning over him and with a distraught expression on her face. 'I'm so sorry. He was being really good, standing on the verge, but when I took that corner, I ran into a pile of wet mud and stones and lost my grip. I skidded into the verge and there he was.'

As Marie stroked his head, she saw Gyp come around slightly and emit a pitiful whine. Her heart was pounding as her brain tried to get into gear. By the time they found a phone and called the vet, it might be too late. 'Do you have a blanket in the car?'

'Yes, yes I do. I'll run and get it.'

The woman and Marie gently eased the blanket under Gyp's limp body. 'If we lift him carefully, it'll be almost as if he's on a stretcher. We can lay him on the back seat of your car, if you don't mind driving me back with him. I've only come from the Manor house — it's about ten minutes down the road.'

The woman drove well considering the shock she had experienced, and as they rounded the bend near Margrave Manor, Marie saw Matthew Hughes tending to the climbing rose at the front of the house. This was no time for her to be distant with Matthew despite their differences. Marie simply got out of the car, explained to him in a few words what had happened and watched him gather Gyp in his arms.

She could see the concern in his dark eyes as he bent his head towards the dog and cradled him like you would a child. 'I'm going to take him to my cottage and lay him down there. He knows it well and it's a bit warmer and quieter than the big house.'

After reassuring the woman driver, and giving her to Mrs Johnson to provide her with a reviving tea, Marie ran off to the cottage to go and check on Gyp.

'How is he?' she asked as Matthew opened the door and walked her through to the lounge.

'I think he'll be OK. It looks like a surface wound. I've washed his leg and I'm just about to bandage it. He's a bit dazed but I think he'll be all right.'

9

Marie stood biting her fingernail as she watched Matthew deftly and with great tenderness lift Gyp's paw and wind the bandage around it. Every now and then, he would stroke the dog's ears and Marie watched Gyp's eyes open as he visibly calmed under Matthew's gentle care. Feeling horribly guilty, Marie did everything she could. Washing up the bowl, making Matthew and her a cup of tea, and finally kneeling down next to the bed Matthew had made up for Gyp on the lounge floor and helping to cover the collie with a clean rug.

'I've called the vet,' said Matthew. 'I know him well, he's going to drop in shortly and make sure we've done the right thing.'

Gyp was asleep now, and Marie said, with a catch in her throat, 'I'd like to stay and see what the vet says, if that's all right.'

'Of course it is,' soothed Matthew.

'If only I had kept him on the lead, or if I'd called out to him sooner to stop him going on the road, perhaps this wouldn't have happened. Lady Margrave's going to be so upset and she's not fully recovered as it is.' Marie sat down, then stood up again, pacing the floor as she spoke.

Matthew turned and instinctively took her in his arms, giving her a reassuring hug. Marie felt so warm and nurtured as he held her, the strength in his arms stilling her shaking body, and yet she could not forget in the back of her mind, her growing suspicions about him having stolen the money and the other items.

She wished she could simply have opened her arms and gained the comfort hugging him back would have given her. But, as she remembered how Sadie Johnson had probably been here, in this very lounge with Matthew only a short while ago, Marie felt an arrow pierce her heart. When Marie didn't reciprocate, but stood like a dead weight in Matthew's arms, she felt him pull away.

His drawing away gave her the sensation of having a warm fire turned off on a winter's day. He knew something was wrong, she could see it in the hurt expression on his face. And yet how on earth could she confront him with her suspicions? She had absolutely no evidence; in fact she could in theory be as much under suspicion as he was.

As the doorbell went, Matthew turned on his heels saying, 'That'll be the vet.'

Once Mr Owen, the vet, had felt the bones in Gyp's paw, shone a light in his eyes, and looked at his gums to gauge the level of shock he said, 'You've done a good job here, Matthew. There are no broken bones, just a flesh wound that will clear up pretty soon. Here are some antibiotics and a few painkillers to help him sleep. He doesn't have concussion so once he's rested he'll be back up on that paw in no time. If you look after him as well as you've done so far, it won't be long before he's running around as usual.'

Shortly after, Lady Margrave called by. 'Thank you, Matthew, for taking him in.'

'I hope I did the right thing, Lady M. To be honest, I was worried about taking him straight back to the Manor and having you see him before I could clean him up. That sort of thing always looks ten times worse when a poor animal's got its fur covered in blood. Once you tidy them up a bit, they're not a such a shock to see.'

Lady Margrave held his hand warmly, 'What would I do without you, Matthew? For a young man, you have a lot of compassion and good judgement.' Matthew offered to make Lady Margrave some tea and show her his garden before he took her back to the Manor so Marie, said her goodbyes.

As she tried to read her book before going to sleep that night, she found her mind constantly going back to the picture of Matthew tending to Gyp. He had been kindness itself. Not even just to the dog who he clearly loved as if he were his own, but to Lady Margrave, he had shown such consideration.

Were those the actions of a thief? Nevertheless, as Marie had walked back and seen the new car sitting in the driveway to Matthew's cottage she was again tortured with questions about where the money had come from for that.

The next day, as Marie was in the morning room fixing a misfeed on the new printer, and Lady Margrave was looking through some old files, Lady Margrave gasped and dropped the papers she was holding.

'What's wrong?' asked Marie, 'you've gone quite pale.'

Lady Margrave looked up at her with an ashen face, and held out a tightly wound bundle of cash, fastened with a rubber band. 'Oh Marie, how on earth could I have forgotten doing that?'

'What?'

'The notes, the money from your plant stall. I remember now, I put them in here.'

Marie put her hand to her mouth; joy mixed with amazement flooded her being. 'Are you sure that's what it is?'

'Yes, I remember now. Do you recall how ill I was feeling when I came into the house that day? There were people everywhere and I'd been on my feet quite a bit. I was exhausted, and I'd had far too much sun. I remember now that when I brought the cash in I was worried about keeping it in too obvious a place so I grabbed a rubber band, wound it around the big bundle of notes and hid them in this file. No one would look there I told myself. Well, you wouldn't would you? I'm so sorry I caused you such a worry.'

'I suppose with the figurine and the painting going missing I didn't even think to question whether I had done

151

something with the money. When I fell to bed that day I felt so tired, and Mrs Johnson kindly gave me various pills to keep my cold at bay but I think they made me terribly drowsy so I forgot all about hiding the money away. If I'd been feeling more myself I would have put it in the safe.'

'Well, there's no harm done and at least we can count it all now, add it to the money I put in the bank the other day, and send a cheque off to the orphanage school with a letter.'

'My, my, at least all's well that end's well as they say.' Lady Margrave sat down heavily in her armchair. 'One thing I am pleased about . . . '

'What's that?'

'That we didn't rush to tell Sam Martin about the money.' When Marie thought about it, she was relieved too. 'Sam seems a nice lad, but he's very ambitious. He's the sort of policeman who needs a result and I think if we had alerted him to the missing money, he would have jumped to conclusions.'

'Do . . . do you think it was Matthew who stole the painting and the figurine?' It was the first time Marie had voiced her concerns out loud. 'I don't want to think wrong of him but it's just that . . . '

'What is it, my dear. Have you seen or heard something that you're not telling me?'

Marie went on to tell Lady Margrave about seeing Sadie Johnson the other night and said that she wondered where Matthew had obtained the money to buy his new car. Lady Margrave looked very serious as she sat in her armchair, her mind ticking over.

'I agree there are things there that don't add up. I've known Matthew for many years now and I would say he has matured a lot over the last few years. I feel the only thing we can do is retain an open mind about him and about Miss Johnson until we learn otherwise, we must not go suspecting people of anything without proper evidence.'

As always, Lady Margrave had been

balanced in her view, thought Marie as she walked through the town later that day to bank the money. She and Lady Margrave were delighted with the final total raised and had composed a letter together to enclose with the cheque for the funds raised. Marie's heart felt lighter than it had for a long time, knowing that Matthew had not in fact stolen the money.

As she came out of the bank and walked back down the main street, to wait for the bus back to Margrave Manor, she was suddenly surprised to see Matthew in the distance. He was outside the police station, standing talking earnestly to DS Sam Martin. Sam and he were having a heated discussion. You wouldn't say it was an argument, but both of them were stating points of view and at one point, Matthew waved his arms then slapped them by his side and strode off to his car.

A wave of nausea spread through Marie as she turned her face towards the bus, which had finally arrived. Why would Matthew be having heated words with Sam Martin? When Marie got back to the house, there was a message from Mrs Johnson on the hall table to say that DS Martin had phoned and would she get in touch with him quickly.

When Marie phoned Sam, he said, 'Good, I'm glad you got back to me so quickly. Marie I'd like to see you. Something has come up in relation to the thefts at Margrave Manor. I'm too busy on something else to see you today but would you be free tomorrow evening.'

'I am free, yes.'

'Good, we'll make a night out of it. Do you like Chinese food?'

'Yes, I do but I don't want to put you to any trouble.'

'It's no trouble. I've missed not seeing you. I can pick you up at the Manor at 7.30 pm., if that's all right.'

'OK, that's fine.'

Marie was a little uncomfortable

about the proposed meeting. Was it business or pleasure? And what were her feelings towards Sam Martin. He seemed very keen and took every opportunity to meet her. But days had gone by and she hadn't heard from him and then suddenly here he was asking our out on what seemed like a proper date. She found it as confusing as she found her feelings towards him and her feelings towards Matthew.

She had been over to see Gyp earlier in the day and had been so touched by the gentle care Matthew was giving to the poor injured dog who seemed to be devoted to Matthew, licking his hand and nuzzling his head at every opportunity. He had endless patience and when she was there, had been tempting Gyp with tidbits to try and encourage the dog to walk a bit and get back to normal.

Marie had felt her heart do a somersault as she watched Matthew. That didn't happen when she was with Sam. But then, Sam seemed so in charge of everything, a man of action and few words. With such a good career and generally acknowledged to be good looking he was the sort of man any girl would be pleased to have interested in her.

Marie knew that had her mother been alive today she would have been delighted to know that Marie was going out with someone as steadfast as Sam. She did her best to be positive about their planned date.

That evening, as Marie was getting ready for bed, she had forgotten the book she was reading and had left it downstairs in the morning room. She was very surprised as she came out, to hear Lady Margrave's voice in the kitchen.

Lady Margrave was usually upstairs and ready for bed at a much earlier hour. Wondering if something was wrong, Marie went towards the kitchen and saw through the door that Lady Margrave was speaking to Matthew who was at the back door.

As she went slowly up the stairs, Marie caught a few words of conversation, as Matthew said to Lady Margrave, 'Don't worry, Lady M. I'll be fine.'

'Well, just you take care of yourself and don't do anything foolish. I'm not sure I agree with this Matthew, but I don't suppose anything I can say will stop you.'

Marie heard Matthew's laugh ring out, as she ascended the stairs not wanting to interfere but wondering what all the plotting was about.

Marie had been asleep for hours when an insistent knocking at her bedroom door, woke her.

At first with her head swimming, squinting at the time on her alarm clock she felt in a daze.

Then she heard Lady Margrave's voice calling to her, 'Marie, Marie, call the police quickly, Matthew has caught our thief.'

Marie grabbed a dressing gown, trying to get her senses together and ran down the stairs so fast, she was sure she did them two at a time. Quickly phoning the police station, they assured her that Sam would be there in no time, with a uniformed constable.

As soon as she put the phone down, Marie ran out into the hall. There, standing by a door in the passageway that Marie had never seen used, stood a plump middle-aged man, his eyes seething with hatred, who had his hands held tightly behind his back by Matthew Hughes, whose other hand was placed firmly on his shoulder.

'Get into the kitchen, Bagshawe,' commanded Matthew who after a brief struggle pinioned the man in a chair, clamping him down all the while.

The older and very unfit intruder was no match for the lean broad-chested Matthew.

Lady Margrave who had followed them down in her night things came into the room and sat opposite the stranger.

'How cold you do this to me, Paul? I never would have thought you would have betrayed me like this. It never occurred to me that our thief might be someone who had worked for me in the past.'

Paul Bagshawe was looking daggers at everyone around him. 'It's all right for you,' he spat, 'you've got this great big house and more money than you know what to do with. You never consider the likes of me when you give us the push, do you?'

'Paul, I couldn't keep you on as a driver you know that. It was your fault you lost your licence through drinking. If you hadn't taken the car out when you were drunk, you would still be working as a chauffeur today.'

'It was your decision to do something that stupid. And now you go and compound it by stealing from me.'

At that point, they heard a car pull up, and men's voices in the driveway. In a moment, Sam and a uniformed policeman burst in at the open kitchen door.

'So,' said Sam looking none too

pleased at Matthew, 'you decided to perform a citizen's arrest, did you?'

'I did. I had a feeling Paul Bagshawe was the culprit and that he would come back for more pickings pretty soon. You may not have believed me, but as you can see, I was right.'

Roughly, Sam and the uniformed policeman stood Paul Bagshawe up and marched him out into the waiting car. As Marie watched them starting the car up, Sam came over to her and said quietly, 'I'm sorry you had to get involved in all this. I told Matthew Hughes I would look into his claim that a former chauffeur had been taking Lady Margrave's possessions but he wouldn't wait. It was a damn fool thing he did to stake out the place and tackle the man like that.'

'Maybe,' said Marie, not sure that it was such a foolish thing to do. Matthew had caught the thief and thank goodness it was all over now. She would reserve her judgement until she got the full facts from Matthew.

'I'll see you later on today, this evening as planned?'

'Maybe,' said Marie, 'call me later, it's been a busy night.'

One thing she did know, she thought as her slippered feet crunched across the gravel, Matthew had been the hero of the moment. He had actually taken some action and they were all a lot safer in their beds now than they had been before. When she got back to the kitchen, Lady Margrave and Matthew were sitting at the kitchen table having a cup of coffee.

"How on earth did you guess it was a former employee who had been stealing?" asked Marie wide eyed, taking her place opposite them and topping up their coffees.

'I didn't,' said Matthew, 'not for certain until I noticed the coal dust on the carpet from the wood store attached to the house. I'm the only one who uses the wood store and I know Mrs Johnson would have my guts for garters if I left any filth on her carpet so I never come into the house that way. But, when I saw the specks of coal dust I knew someone had.

'I also knew that the door from the wood store leads straight into the house and that that must be the weak point where the thief had entered. I spoke to Lady Margrave and when I told her my suspicions she confirmed that the front and back door keys were always changed when there was a change of staff but no-one thought about the wood store keys.'

'Initially I kept my thoughts to myself, but when I was more sure I was right, I tried to tell Sam Martin, but he didn't seem too keen on any information I had. I think he'd decided from the beginning it was either myself, Mrs Johnson or someone associated with one of us. I didn't know Paul Bagshawe well, he got sacked only a couple of weeks after I came to work here but it was purely by chance I ran into him.'

'Ran into him?'

'Yes, the day I went to the car

auction. I was left some money by an aunt, it wasn't a big legacy but as my car would have cost a fortune to repair, I decided to spend the legacy on a new car. When I was at the auction, walking around I suddenly heard Gyp growling.'

Marie was listening, enthralled and jumped in with, 'that's right, I remember you took Gyp with you that day.'

'Poor Gyp, the moment he saw Paul Bagshawe, he bared his teeth and started growling at the man. I had to rack my brain to think who he was. It wasn't until much later, when I'd got back to the Manor I remembered where I'd seen that face before. Then, suddenly it all began to slot back into place. Gyp's a good guard dog and would have raised the alarm if a complete stranger had come into the house, but of course he knew Paul Bagshawe.'

'What's more, I have a strong suspicion that on the odd occasion, Paul had mistreated Gyp. I've never seen that dog cower before anyone, but if Paul had raised his hand to him in the past, Gyp would have remembered. That explained why Gyp didn't raise the alarm.'

'I see, and I realise now why Paul Bagshawe didn't take a load of stuff all at once. If he's in the second-hand car trade, it's easier to 'launder' any takings from a robbery if you do it little and often and he probably felt that he could dip in to this house at any time to top up his earnings and that the police would never know where the extra cash came from.'

'Exactly.'

As they talked, Marie marvelled at Matthew. He talked animatedly to Lady Margrave as if it had been a bit of an adventure, without a thought for the danger he might have put himself in. She watched as his bright brown eyes lit up as he related to Lady Margrave how he'd worked everything out in his mind.

The old lady beamed a smile up at him and every now and then touched his arm as if she couldn't believe it was all real. All the things Marie had suspected Matthew of were untrue, how could she have judged him so badly? If only Sam Martin had let her in on Matthew's suspicions, she would not have treated him so unkindly.

Then, Marie remembered Sadie coming out of Matthew's cottage, and her heart plummeted. Of course Sadie was seeing him, why wouldn't she? After all, Matthew was good looking, fun to be with, loyal and hard working. Lucky Sadie, thought Marie, finding it difficult to swallow her coffee with the lump she felt in her throat.

Eventually, they all said goodnight to each other, and Marie told Matthew she would update Mrs Johnson when Mrs Johnson came in in the morning.

⋆ ⋆ ⋆

When she woke up, Marie's heart was heavy. She felt dreadfully guilty at ever suspecting Matthew of being the thief and, as soon as she heard Mrs Johnson's key in the lock, Marie ran down to tell her what had happened.

'Well, I never.' Mrs Johnson looked out of the kitchen window in the direction of Matthew's cottage. 'I've misjudged that young man.'

'You have?'

'Yes, cruelly misjudged him in fact. Once or twice, I was convinced he was the thief and then, on top of all of that when I thought my Sadie was seeing him I really turned against him.'

Mrs Johnson flopped down into a kitchen chair, tugging the tea towel she held agitatedly in her hands and Marie sat opposite her, while it all poured out.

'You see, the thing is, Sadie had a good boyfriend, a lad called Gary. She seemed very keen on Gary and I hoped finally she might settle down. Then, all of a sudden she started asking me about Matthew Hughes. She seemed to have a sort of crush on him. I thought she was two timing Gary when I found out she'd been to Matthew's cottage.'

'What I didn't realise was that the foolish girl had had a major tiff with Gary and she was looking for someone to be seen with and to spread rumours about to get Gary jealous so they could get back together again. In actual fact, she pursued Matthew even when he told her in no uncertain terms he wasn't interested. If I'm honest, Marie, I think he's pretty interested in you although he doesn't know how to say it.'

Marie's heart filled with joy as she heard Mrs Johnson's words. 'Oh, I don't know about that, Mrs Johnson.'

'Well then, you must be blind young lady if you haven't seen the way he looks at you. Can't take his eyes off you. What's more, you'd be much better off with Matthew than that po-faced policeman Sam Martin.'

'I would?'

'You do know, that Sam Martin is engaged, don't you?'

10

Marie felt as if she had been slapped in the face. Now everything began to make sense. 'Engaged!'

'That's right. I'm not surprised he hasn't told you. They've been engaged for ages. Her mother belongs to my WI group. The girl's name is Naomi. Apparently the poor girl's wanted to get married for ages, but he'll never name the day. If you ask me, that young man's got a roving eye.'

'Thank you for telling me,' Marie felt completely shell-shocked, but also, suddenly light headed. Matthew hadn't been dating Sadie Johnson. In fact it sounded as if he'd been trying nicely to get rid of her. Marie got up and pushed her chair in. 'I have something I must do.'

Marie marched off to the morning room, sat down at the desk and dialled

Sam's number. Her heart was pounding with trepidation as she listened to the connection as it clicked through.

'Sam Martin.' His voice was hard, businesslike.

'Hi Sam, it's Marie.'

'Marie, it's really nice to hear from you.'

Marie stiffened in her chair as she heard Sam's voice soften into a sort of croon as he spoke, all charm when he knew it was her. He continued, 'I hope you can still make it this evening after all that excitement during the night. I still think it would have been better if Matthew Hughes had left the detective work up to us . . . '

Sam really could be two different people, a Mister Jekyll and Mister Hyde character. Marie realised with a jolt he had been that all along. One minute nice the next minute not. And anyone who could deceive their fiancée by sneaking around with another woman made her squirm. Marie was only too happy that she hadn't let Sam get any further with his attentions towards her.

'Actually Sam,' she interrupted him, 'I won't be coming out with you this evening.' There was an uncomfortable pause. 'Or ever again.'

Silence ticked down the line until he said, 'Why not?'

It was difficult for Marie, she hated confrontation, but she breathed in and said, 'I think you know why, Sam. You remember that night when we were out at the concert, and your friend asked you where Naomi was. Well, I believe you lied to me that day.'

'I . . . She . . . We're not getting on too well.'

'But she's your fiancée, isn't she, Sam?'

'Like I said, we're not getting on, haven't been for some time.'

'Well, I really think you ought to work out your problems in a different way, Sam, or you're going to end up hurting a lot of people. She's still your fiancée, you haven't denied that, and I don't want to get mixed up in anything like that, thank you. Goodbye, Sam.' Marie jammed the phone down firmly in its cradle and stood up.

She was trembling slightly but at least she had been honest even if Sam couldn't. Marie came out of the morning room knowing what she wanted to do now. She had to go and see Matthew before she lost him, the one thing which was possibly the best thing that had happened to her in ages. Grabbing her jacket, she went into the kitchen.

'Mrs Johnson, I have to go out.'

'Before you do,' Mrs Johnson got up and came over to Marie, putting her hand on the girl's arm. 'As we were having a bit of a heart to heart just now, I realised I have to give you an apology.'

'You do?'

'Yes, I do. I wasn't too kind to you when you first came here. In fact I resented you terribly. I didn't think Lady Margrave needed a secretary. You see, I'd done little things to try and help her keep her affairs together, posting letters and helping her file stuff and all that. And I thought I had taken on a sort of role as a companion. I thought, well, I thought maybe you'd try and take my place.'

'I could never do that, Mrs Johnson.' Marie laughed even to think of the idea. 'You run this household like a well-oiled machine, I couldn't begin to do all the things you do and cook such fantastic meals and keep everything as bright and clean as a new pin. And besides, Lady Margrave looks on you as an old friend. Nothing will ever change that.'

'Well, I just wanted to say that I'm pleased you're here now. That fund-raising day was delightful. To see the gardens full of people again like they used to be and having folks admiring the flowers and saying how delicious my cakes were was like a real breath of fresh air.'

'Thank you.' Marie held the other woman's hands briefly in hers, and thought what a nice smile Mrs Johnson had when she chose to use it. 'Now, I really must go and deal with some unfinished business.' Marie blushed from her toes to her ears, 'Matthew said that Gyp could come back today, so I'm going over to the cottage to fetch him.'

Mrs Johnson gave her a knowing smile and watched as Marie, in her white T-shirt and jacket and flowered skirt ran out of the house towards Matthew's. Marie's feet took her quickly along the driveway to his cottage until it was nearly in sight. Then she found herself slowing down, as self-doubt crept into her mind. How would Matthew greet her now?

She had treated Matthew pretty shabbily the other day. She had suspected him of thieving and had thought the worst of him when Sadie Johnson had been playing her silly games. She had been blind to Sam Martin's duplicity and at times thought him the better man just because he had a high-flying job and all the trappings like money to take her on evenings out and a nice car.

All along, Matthew had shown nothing but caring and kindness and yet she'd doubted him. Marie wondered, as she gingerly knocked on the cottage door whether Matthew would really want to see her again.

'Marie,' his brown eyes looked enquiringly at her.

'Hello, Matthew. I've come to ... ' She wanted to say so many things to him and yet now she was here it was much more difficult than she'd imagined. Her heart was in her mouth as she struggled to find the words. 'I ... I've come to see Gyp, to take him back home.'

The dog was sitting up in the bed Matthew had so carefully made for him. Gyp stood up, wagged his tail and looked from Matthew to Marie and back to Matthew again. 'I think maybe he wants to stay here with you. You've looked after him so well, Matthew.'

'I only did what anyone would have

done in the circumstances.' For once, Matthew looked less than his usual confident self. They hadn't been alone together for a while and Marie could feel that the air was heavy with unsaid words.

'No you didn't, Matthew.' Marie knew it was now or never. She had this one chance to make everything right. 'You did much, much more than you had to. You always do.'

He looked questioningly at her, his hands by his sides, his mouth opened as if he wanted to say something but she couldn't let him, she had to say her piece while she still had the courage. 'You've been so good, Matthew, to Gyp, to Lady Margrave, to me.'

'I wanted you to feel at home here,' he said.

'Well, you certainly did that. And I've realised over the short time I've been here that everything you do, you do for other people. I'm . . . I'm,' Marie stuttered, her hands damp with sweat, tears pricking the back of her eyes, 'I'm so sorry, I admit I doubted you at some point, Matthew. I thought you might be the thief, I . . . '

Matthew came towards her, hesitated, then put his hands gently on her shoulders, 'Of course you did. I was a chief suspect, wasn't I? I think we all suspected each other at some point. That's why this whole nasty business has been difficult for all of us. You only thought what anyone would have done in your position, Marie. But I'm so glad it's all cleared up now and we can get to know each other properly.'

'You do still want to get to know me then?' Marie felt her spirits rise as she allowed herself to hope.

'I believe I do.' Then a seriousness clouded his face, as he held her firmly in his strong hands. 'One thing I have to know.'

'What's that?'

'What's going on between you and Sam Martin?'

'Nothing!' declared Marie. 'Absolutely nothing.' She went on to relate the revelation about Sam's fiancee and told Matthew about her phone call this morning to tell Sam she would never be seeing him again.

As her words poured out in a flood, she saw Matthew's expression change. That wide, boyish smile which spread like the sunlight over his whole face was turned on her and he said, 'I'm so glad, Marie. I couldn't be more glad because I think, no, I know, I'm falling in love with you.'

With that, he took her in his arms, drew her to him and she felt herself melt into his kiss as she tangled her fingers in the soft curls at the back of his neck. At last, as Marie moulded herself into Matthew's embrace, she felt she had come home, to the place she wanted to stay, forever.